BEAUTIFUL PIECE

BEAUTIFUL PIECE

Joseph G. Peterson

Northern Illinois University Press
DeKalb

Published by the Northern Illinois University Press, DeKalb,
Illinois 60115

Design by Shaun Allshouse

Library of Congress Cataloging-in-Publication Data

Peterson, Joseph G.

Beautiful piece / Joseph G. Peterson.

p. cm.

ISBN 978-0-87580-629-7 (pbk.: alk. paper)

I. Title.

PS3616.E84288B43 2009

813'.6—dc22

2009017669

To Rachel, my North Star

With gratitude to
Tracy Schoenle and
Shaun Allshouse
for their collaboration
on this project

WE ALWAYS FALL ASLEEP SMOKING one more cigarette in bed. Just one more, I'll say, or she'll say, and with lights out in the room, one more, and we'll light one more cigarette, sharing it in the dark, watching the ember glow, and when we're done, we'll carefully nub it out, reaching with our hands to find the ashtray in the dark.

Her mattress is on the floor of her apartment—she's never owned a bed, apparently—and her place, like mine, and the Vet's, for that matter, is a wreck. This doesn't give her any pride, but she's too busy, she says, to do anything about it. Take me as I come, she said, when she first let me into her apartment and I saw the place strewn with stuff. She stripped naked almost immediately, and I did as she asked: I took her as she came. Hers is a one-bedroom apartment. Books scattered everywhere. Shoes piled up in the closet. Clothes lying about—thrown on top of the hamper or the radiator or hanging from the doorknobs. All sorts of barrettes and ribbons for her hair scattered on her dresser top. She has one window, which peeks out onto the alley. She keeps it propped open with a broomstick in the summer months, and a simple roll-down shade provides privacy when privacy is needed. The first time we slept together (that was when she said take me as I come) was OK. It was more of a disappointment for her than for me, I suppose. She broke out in garish laughter, but I grinned and bore it. Not much else to report there. Occasionally a mysterious smile flashes across her face—which makes me proud as hell—and the thing is it contains a mystery that only darkness, night, and the intimacy of bed reveal.

At the time we met, she was with another guy, Matthew Gliss, whom I vaguely knew. I didn't know why or how I knew him, which is why I say I vaguely knew him—but he seemed like a good guy and he was always slapping me on my back when he saw me. She and Matthew were engaged to be married long before I ever met her. In fact I knew they were engaged when I took her as she came. I don't exactly know why I agreed to sleep with her that first afternoon we were together. I suppose I was feeling like an opportunist, and I hated to let a good thing pass—especially something that seemed so easy. But you know, Matthew's picture was all over her place. She had a picture of him on her dresser, and in a glass-enclosed bookcase were several photos of them snapped in happier times—both of them smiling, well dressed, healthy, and each with a mouthful of good teeth. When I first saw pictures of him in her place, I told her I knew him. When she asked how, I told her I really didn't know how but he looked familiar and I was certain I had bought him drinks at one point or another. Later, while we were in the sack making love—when she was presenting me with that garish laugh of hers—I felt like hell to be taking her away from him—especially since he seemed to like me. At least I remember him liking me. Those were my impressions of him—that he liked me, even though even now those impressions remain and are becoming increasingly vague. I also recall he was a decent guy, but what do I know? What's more, this thing with Lucy, I mean our relationship, hell, it had just started up. I didn't have a feeling for her one way or the other, really. I mean the whole thing was easy—we actually met at a gas station. I helped her with her credit card, which appeared not to be working at the pump. I double swiped it for her, and boom, just like that, she was ready to gas up. While she stood at the pump pumping her car, which was a Mazda RX-7, and while I stood at the pump pumping my AMC Hornet, I caught her watching me out the corner of her eye. I suppose she can just as easily say she caught me watching her out the corner of my eye. In any event we started talking about some inane subject—like the weather—and before I knew it, she asked what I was doing just now.

What are your plans? she asked.

None to speak of, I said. And it was true. I had only driven my car to the gas station to gas it up. After that, I intended to drive back home and do whatever it was I was doing before I decided to gas up my car.

Wanna come over to my place for drinks?

It was hot as hell, I was thirsty, and what's more I was curious. So I said—I think these were my exact words—What the hell. She gave me directions to her place. I in fact followed her home. She lives in a rather decrepit apartment complex that has a derelict swimming pool, which long ago had been given up to the wear of time and waste of weather. I parked my car next to hers, we ascended the two flights of rusted iron steps, and she opened the door to her tiny place. That's when, turning to me, she said: This is it—take me as I come. Promptly she tore off her clothes, and like I say, I did my best and took her as she came.

That was our beginning. I don't think I've ever heard of a relationship with a more inane beginning. Take me as I come. So I took her. Garish laughter ensued. I grinned and bore it. Meanwhile there were my doubts about the man in the pictures, whom I recalled was a reasonably decent guy, though for the life of me I couldn't recall why I thought him decent or even how I knew him.

Afterwards, we did what I least like to do: we lie there in bed and talked about it. It was hot in her room, so she propped her window open with that broomstick and poked the fan switch with her toe, and the fan blew hot air across our elongated or foreshortened or overheated bodies and I noticed my fingertips still smelled of gasoline—that's how little time elapsed from the moment I first saw her until lying naked with her in bed—while she, cigarette in hand, began to regale me with sundry stories of her life. One, for example, always recurred whenever we were naked—recurred, that is, until the situation changed entirely, thereby removing the issue that compelled the story in the first place. She began talking of it almost as soon as I had withdrawn from her and rolled over on my side of the bed to catch my breath. That's when she lit up her cigarette and began to talk.

I've been engaged to Matthew fourteen months now, she said, in her way. No wedding date is in sight, she continued, in her way. I don't know how long we've been together. Forever, I suppose. But do me a favor. If he ever walks through those doors and sees you here with me, get out as soon as possible. Run, don't walk, and hide. If you give him a chance to catch you he will probably most likely also want to kill you.

Hearing this surprised me because I remember Matthew Gliss as being a rather decent guy. But when she told me that he'd be murderous if he caught me I was scared. I mean irrationally scared. I asked myself that moment, I remember saying to myself: Have I stepped unwittingly into a hornet's nest? Maybe this wasn't such a good idea after all to come here after gassing up my car. It's a bad omen. Maybe I should have stuck to my plan and declined her offer.

What are you doing right now?

No plans to speak of. . . . Wait, I have a few things to do around the house. Why?

Because if you want to cool off with a drink at my place you're welcome to come.

No, no, I'm fine, thank you.

In fact I had no intention of intruding on this guy's woman. I no more wanted to take her than I wanted to rob a bank. But the vault was open so to speak, and there was money on the table, and no one was watching, so why not rob the bank? I needed the cash anyway and it was a perfectly simple thing to do. So when she said, Want to come home with me? I thought, Why the hell not? I can rob that bank. No one's looking. It would be easy as pie. And it was easy as pie, until now. My hands still smell like gasoline and I'm worried I might have stepped on a hornet's nest. It was a bad omen.

She tells me he'll kill me. Her toe is touching the back of my calf and the fan is blowing hot air across our elongated or foreshortened bodies. I remember distinctly asking myself, Why would a decent guy like Matthew Gliss—someone I vaguely remember as being a nice guy—want to kill me? And once I'm dead, I thought, that's it. No more me. Everything that I am will be gone. Except for the memory of me—the memory that my mom and dad have of me. The memory that the Vet and Epstein have of me. The memory that a few other characters may have of me—particularly Addison, who runs Sal's. Whenever I'm at Sal's, Addison is always buying me a brandy and smiling on my progress. You're progressing beautifully in life, he likes to tell me. I'm proud of you. Cheers. Or he'll simply say, Enjoy, enjoy. Addison is always telling me to enjoy myself. He's protective of me. Enjoy, he says, putting food in front of me. No rush to pay. Just enjoy yourself. I love him like a grandfather. He's met Lucy a few times but he's mum on what he thinks of her. Enjoy, he says. Enjoy the time you have with her. You never know when it may all be over.

I have no intention of taking Matthew Gliss's girl. That's not what this is about, I tell myself. This is not about taking somebody else's girl. I have absolutely no intention of taking another person's girl.

I'm lying there in the sack when she tells me for the first time that Matthew Gliss will kill me if he catches me. I recall him being a nice guy, like I say, though for the life of me I don't know why I thought he was nice—he certainly looked nice in those pictures, and like I say, I had a vague memory of him, a positive memory. I mean my impression of him was that he seemed to like me. So when she said, Watch out, he may walk in any moment, and if he finds you here he may kill you, I naturally asked, Well, does he have a key to the place? And if he has a key does he have a gun?

Of course he does. He has a key and a gun. I gave him a key just after we got engaged. He's always had a gun, but he didn't show it to me until after I agreed to marry him. When I agreed to marry him, he immediately showed me his gun. A 10mm Glock automatic is what he calls it. It's fearsome. I've seen him fire it at abandoned cars and the damage it did to the steel was incredible.

Do you expect him home soon or do I have time?

I'd say you have some time. He's working right now. Though sometimes he comes home early, and if he comes home early today then I'd say you better run, don't walk, when he comes in through the door.

How much time do we have left until he comes home—that is, if he doesn't come home early?

About enough time to smoke another cigarette, and then you should probably be going.

I lit a cigarette and offered her one: One more? I asked, holding the cigarette out.

Sure.

And so began our little ritual: Lights out, one more, and there we'd lie in the dark, sharing a cigarette, watching the ember burn in the dark. Only the first time we did it, it wasn't night, but day, hot as hell, the fan blowing hot air across our foreshortened or elongated bodies.

ONE DAY HE DID COME HOME early from work and like she promised he tried to kill me. At least I think he tried to kill me. That at least is how I interpreted his intent. Lucy and I had only been together a few weeks. At that point, I felt like absolute hell. She had changed her allegiance over to me almost completely. I sensed she still had vestigial loyalties to Matthew, but for one reason or another—which I couldn't entirely explain—I sensed that she was finding me more companionable than Matthew despite the fact that she was engaged to him and had only met me a few weeks earlier in the summer. Again, it wasn't my intention to take her away from Matthew. Hell, if things were reversed, if it had been him in the sack and me on the outside looking in, I might have felt similar to him. I might have inadvertently burst in on them and tried to kill him. Though I didn't own a Glock automatic. In principal I avoid guns like I avoid the plague.

One day I was sitting with the Vet and explained: You see the problem with guns as I see it is.

You need a gun? he asked me.

No no. Quite the contrary. I avoid guns like the plague. It's my theory guns only attract guns. Shooting begets shooting. Do you see what I'm saying?

Whatever. You need me to collect you a gun, I'll collect you a gun. Just let me know.

I don't want a gun, I tell him. I avoid guns like the plague. I wouldn't own a gun even if you collected one for me.

Whatever, says the Vet. Just let me know. You need it, I'll get it. How about that?

Fine, I say. That sounds fine.

SO SHE SAYS TO ME: He has a Glock 10mm automatic is what he calls it. It's fearsome. I've seen him fire it at abandoned cars and the damage it did to the steel was incredible.

To which I say, Odd, a gun. I wouldn't own a gun even if I could.

Good, she says. I hate guns.

FOR THE LIFE OF ME, I could not recall how I knew Matthew Gliss. Interestingly, ever since the day I met Lucy at the gas station, I never saw Matthew again, except in those pictures—the one on the dresser and the ones in the bookcase that were always staring down on us, the ones where they're smiling with their beautiful teeth—and of course there was that time I saw him when he inadvertently barged in on us and threatened to kill me. I remember that moment vividly—run, don't walk—and as he burst through the door, I remember looking up from the bedsheets where she and I were lying, thinking: Who is this guy? Is that him? It must be him. He looked vaguely familiar, though for some reason he looked nothing like the guy in all those photos—the guy who, staring down at me with those beautiful teeth, always made me feel terrible for taking his girl away from him.

Is that him? I asked in the confusion of the moment.

It's him. Run, don't walk!

It looks nothing like him.

It's him.

It doesn't even look anything like the man I vaguely remember—the man who used to slap me on the back every time I saw him. The man I bought beers for one time or another.

It's him.

And so it was him, and between the moment he burst through the door and the moment he stepped into the bedroom to get a closer look at me, I had time enough to think a thousand thoughts. Not to mention my mind drifted back to that moment, several weeks earlier when, standing at the gas pump, I caught her staring at me and she caught me staring at her—and she, being quicker on the move than I, told me she was having a problem with her credit card and would I mind horribly. It was hot as hell. I wasn't doing a thing that day. Just minding my own business. In fact I had arrived at the gas station to gas up my car. Then I was going to go back home and do more chores or lie around the house perhaps. I had no plans for the day—or for the rest of my life for that matter. I was a man without a plan, and the days melted into years—and it went on like this for many years—me puttering around my apartment with nothing much to do—or lying around on the couch caught in a vicious take-no-prisoners cycle of tube watching or occasionally going out with the Vet to a bar or to the racetrack or fishing with Epstein in the river—and when we went fishing we usually fished in the Des Plaines River for carp. And when we caught the carp, instead of keeping the fish, we unhooked them. We were always very gentle with the fish we caught. It was like they were sacred to us, and I can't explain why we treated the fish as if they were sacred beings to us. Had I fished alone for carp or had Epstein fished alone for carp each of us might have felt differently. We might have treated the carp like the rough fish that they were. Though I probably would have been more inclined to treat the carp roughly than Epstein, for Epstein is first and foremost a mystic—that is, he relates mystically to the world, in a positive manner. Oneness, that sort of thing. I, on the other hand, am forever dividing things, breaking them down. Epstein, on the other hand, is forever putting things back together. Putting things together that don't even belong together. Mixing things up and, finally, finding beauty and joy and happiness and harmony in the chaos of it. So together we had this bond. It was part of how we viewed life—more so Epstein than I—and I say this because I feel I always viewed life differently while I was with Epstein than when I was away from him. I felt as if the world and all of its living creatures were just a little more holy and sacred than we, and so, accordingly, we treated the world's creatures with tremendous deference. The carp, for instance, were sacred beings to us in an immaculate sort of way. Even though the carp were rough fish, we treated them as if they were the most holy of fish—as if they were the rare arctic grayling. We caught them on hooks baited with corn or with stink bait, and we gingerly netted them as if their coats of scales weren't the most durable coats of scales known to fish—for carp, it is known, can survive nearly a whole day out of water in the baking sun. But we treated them as if they were the most delicate of god's good creatures. We netted them with great delicacy. Quickly we pulled the steel from their round and rubbery mouths—as if we were dislodging a thorn from the tender foot of a child. Carpe diem, he would say or I would say. And then we would gently let the carp go and always I was amazed the moment the stunned carp went back into the river, then a twitch of the tail, a swirl of water, and it was gone, re-merged with the murky depths. And I would turn and say to Epstein: Can you believe they call these rough fish?

And Epstein would say: There's nothing rough about them.

So when she said, Can you help me with this credit card—it doesn't seem to be working? I naturally thought, Why not? She was an island in an ocean, and I was tired of swimming. She was a piece of driftwood floating in my direction. Or, perhaps, I was a piece of driftwood floating in hers. In any event, when we saw each other floating aimlessly out there in the open water of that hot summer day we naturally gravitated towards each other. Excuse me, my card is not working—can you help me? She could have asked the gas station attendant, but she asked me instead. My hunch at the time was that her card was working. She was only looking for an excuse to make contact with me. First she saw me seeing her, then I saw her seeing me, or the other way around, and then her card wasn't working, even though it was, so I stepped over the berm that naturally separated us, I swiped her card a couple of times, and presto, just like that she began pumping her car and I went back to pumping mine, and that's when our rather inane conversation began.

Hot, huh?

Yes.

I suppose it'll get worse.

I suppose so.

It always gets worse before it gets better.

Isn't that the truth, I said, trying hard not to pay attention to anything in particular.

But the thing is, it—our inane conversation—masked this other thing, which wasn't so inane—this thing that was happening to us. For there we both out in the open water, swimming to keep afloat though for the life of us we were sinking fast—our arms too exhausted with the swim. Who knows how long I'd been swimming out there in the water, no land in sight, not an island, not even a piece of driftwood, the carp swimming up alongside my legs. And I was tired of swimming. I was tired of the monotony of it. The monotony of alternately swimming and floating and the ever present terror of death by drowning. She was swimming too. She was, like me, in over her head. No land or anything of the sort was in sight. But she saw me and I saw her and we both saw immediately that we were nothing more than pieces of old driftwood floating in the open water, no land in sight, and what a relief it was to see something, anything, out there in the open ocean water, especially another person, especially her. And that line by Coleridge. I couldn't get it out of my head: Water water everywhere and not a drop to drink. Only I would substitute the word 'beer' when I wasn't actually in Sal's but desiring to be there: Water water everywhere but not a beer to drink. And before I knew it—we touched out there in the open water.

My card's not working.

I stepped over the berm that naturally separated us and she offered me a drink.

You want to come over to my house for a drink and cool off? You look thirsty as hell.

I was thirsty as hell. Water water everywhere. I could have gone to my own place and had a drink. My fridge was loaded with pop, not to mention beer. But it was hot as hell and suffering in the heat when you're by yourself only seems to make the heat worse. What's more, I had nothing else to do—but perhaps call Epstein and spend the early evening drinking beers and fishing. What's more, I no more wanted to take her than I wanted to rob a bank but the bank vault was suddenly opened and there was the money on the table. Whole stacks of cash. And who was I to say no—when a bank vault inadvertently opened—and there was no one around and the temptation to take it was so strong? Go ahead: Take the money. Nobody is around. The money is yours. No one will ever know you took it. So I did. Why the hell not? That's what I remember asking myself: Why the hell not? And when no answer was forthcoming—when the only answer that came to mind was: Epstein can fish by himself tonight—when I could not think of a reason not to go home with her, I assented.

Sure, I told her, why the hell not? And off we went—she in her car and I in mine.

I followed her in her car to her apartment complex. It was a derelict place—so dirty and unkempt. I thought it was a bad omen when I saw it. I distinctly remember saying to myself, This is a bad omen. This place is too derelict. Surely it's a bad omen. But the cash was on the table and no one was looking. So this is where she lives, I thought. And I remember trying to take a forgiving tact: Your place is no better than hers, don't forget. That's what I told myself. You're no better than she is, so don't turn your nose up at it. And I was right. My place was no better than hers. Nevertheless, when I saw her place, I thought it was a bad omen. And what do you think she'd think of your place? I asked myself as I followed her up the stairs to her place. She'd probably think it's a bad omen. Which raises the question: What does it say about her, if, upon meeting me at the gas station, she had agreed to go home to my place? What does it say about me that, instead, I'm going to hers? Nevertheless, I couldn't resist. I had nothing better to do. What's more, Epstein could fish alone.

As we climbed the steps to her place, I thought: What a cunning place to put a bank vault. And it was true. No one was looking. There was a swimming pool. But it had been abandoned to the whim of time and the wear of weather and as I went up the steps I surveyed the place. I hope no one sees me, I thought. It was irrational that I should be so paranoid all of a sudden, because you see, this thing was so easy. In fact it couldn't have been easier, so why worry about it? I hope no one sees me, I said again, to myself. And that's when she opened the door to her place, took her top off, pointed to the mess of stuff strewn about and said: Take me as I come.

THE SMELL IN HER PLACE wasn't fetid like I thought it might be. Though sometime thereafter the smell did become fetid—and when it became fetid I said to myself: This is a bad omen. Maybe I shouldn't be here. When it became fetid I said to myself—I distinctly remember saying—What am I doing here?

Nonetheless, that first time, the very first time I stepped into her place, something happened between us. She was no longer simply an open vault. Instead she was a beach to rest upon. A tropical beach, perhaps, or perhaps a beach in the city like the North Avenue Beach, for example, or like any of the other public beaches up and down the shore of Lake Michigan. It didn't matter, but it was a beach upon which I could rest myself, too weary from swimming alone in the open sea.

I'm happy to have found a beach, I told Epstein one day.

Yes.

After swimming so long by myself.

Surely it must be a relief.

I had fallen in love to be sure. At least I think I had fallen in love. I remember asking myself: Am I falling in love here? Is this what's happening? Is this what this is all about—love? But I told myself: No—it's about the bank vault, because the day we first met, everything was so easy. It was simple as pie, really. And that's why I did it to begin with. Because it was simple as pie. When she asked, Do you want to come home with me? I hesitated, but it was hot as hell and she was offering and the whole thing was so easy. It was simple as pie. So why the hell not? I remember distinctly saying to myself. Why the hell not?

Do you want to come to my place for a drink?

Why the hell not?

I didn't go to her place for any other reason than it was simple as pie. Then there were the bad omens, all the obvious ones, not to mention all the ancillary ones, which would pop up soon enough, bad omens that I had to overlook if I were to carry on with this thing, and overlooking the bad omens, though not easy as pie, was nevertheless, I found, quite doable. And as I overlooked all the bad omens, one day passed into another, and the hot summer, which never ceased, remained a hot summer. And all those summer weeks we read about how the heat wave was destroying the elderly and the sick and the infirm and the poor and how emergency rooms were piling up with corpses and refrigerated meatpacking trucks were parked outside hospitals to accommodate all the corpses so they wouldn't rot in the heat and the city morgues too were filled to the breaking point with corpses, for it was the worst heat wave of the century and the city wasn't prepared for the worst heat wave of the summer. And all the people who died from the heat wave died alone, for there is something about being alone in the heat—it makes the heat worse. So even though I had plans—even though I had only come to the gas station to gas up my car, even though I had plans to go back to my place and do what I had planned to do—I didn't want to face my hot apartment alone. It's perfectly understandable, I tell myself now, that you should have gone to her place. Perfectly understandable that you didn't go back home to your apartment alone in the heat. So while we were gassing up our cars and she asked, What are you doing right now? I responded, No plans. And so off we went: she in her RX-7 and I in my AMC Hornet. And ascending the rusted iron stairs to her place, I distinctly remember looking over my shoulder, looking out onto the derelict parking lot, out upon the abandoned pool thinking: This is a bad omen. But it was hot as hell and when you are alone in the heat, the heat is unbearable. Let me tell you, you have no idea. And that summer hundreds of people were dying. They were falling like flies in the pent-up, fetid air of their closed apartments. It was a bad omen. The whole thing was a bad omen. And I didn't want to die like this. Alone in my own apartment, for I was always alone in my apartment. Whole weeks would pass and there I would be for whole weeks, alone in my apartment. Alone in the heat and absolutely alone. If I were to suddenly die, in the middle of the night, as it were, I would tell myself time to time, it would be weeks before anyone discovered me. The problem with living alone, I thought, is that you can live alone so long that people grow accustomed to you living alone. They stop bothering you, really. That was the whole trouble with living alone. People got used to you living alone and they would slowly but surely stop bothering about how you are getting along all alone in your apartment alone. It was a real problem that each of us living alone had to deal with. So that if suddenly you should stop living, if you should die—suddenly—alone in your apartment, it could be weeks before anyone discovered your body. As a result one had to adopt methods, survival methods. For example, a method I adopted was I would force myself to wake in the middle of the night, just to check and make sure I was still alive. Living alone in your apartment by yourself is unnatural. I came to see that living alone was an unnatural state. I would spend whole weeks living alone, and I would curse—to myself, of course—about how unnatural it was to be stuck in my apartment all alone. Alone in the hot fetid air. I would curse and then I would grow paranoid. What if I were to die suddenly, in the middle of the night? How would anyone ever know? What if I died alone in the hot fetid air and my body were to lie undiscovered until the odor of rot was overwhelming, forcing someone to break open the door? And when I had thoughts like these, I would become enraged. It doesn't seem right, I would say to myself. It doesn't seem right that I should be alone in my apartment and the only way they would find my body is from the fetid smells emanating from my rotting corpse. How is it some people manage to shack up, and others—people like me who had the best of intentions—ended up alone? I would look at myself in the mirror and say to myself, You have the best of intentions. You could be a wonderful husband, a spouse, a family man. You have much to give. But here you are all alone in your apartment. Abandoned so to speak. Discarded, so to speak. Alone so long, no one bothers to check in on you time to time.

DURING THAT TIME OF MY LIFE, everything seemed like a bad omen. It was a terrible omen that I was even talking to myself in the mirror. Addressing myself in the second person. Surely, I said to myself, this can't be a good omen. You're talking to yourself in the second person. So I made arrangements with friends. I made arrangements with the Vet, who also lived alone, directly above my apartment. He had a gimp leg from a war wound and banged around all day and all night long directly above me. It was reassuring, always reassuring, to hear his foot banging on the floorboards above my apartment. It was always good to know at least someone was there. I called the Vet and explained my plan to him.

What if I should die suddenly in the middle of the night, as it were? Alone, as it were! Who would discover me? I have been living alone so long, people have stopped checking in on me to see how I'm doing.

He understood.

I understand, he said.

Let's make a pact, I said, and so we made a pact between us to check in on each other regularly. He would knock on my door once in a while if he hadn't heard from me or I would knock on his door once in a while if I hadn't heard from him.

Let's not wait until we smell the corpse on this one.

That would be ignominious, he said, and the Vet actually used that word: 'ignominious.' It was a lovely word, really, and I agreed with him.

It would be ignominious, I said, using his lovely word. In this heat, you wouldn't have to be dead long before the smells became unbearable. It would be ignominious.

I'd hate to have to discover your corpse because it was rotting, he said, reiterating my concern. Have you ever smelled a dead corpse?

As opposed to a living corpse? I asked.

It's ignominious, he said. But I tried to cut him off at the pass, for as soon as an opportunity presented itself for the Vet to talk about the corpses of his war experience, he took it. He took his opportunity and he would run with it, and once he started running with his war experiences there was no telling where he would end up. There were plenty of corpses in his war experience so there were any number of directions he might run with it. He might end up laughing irrationally or crying rationally. Or laughing rationally and crying irrationally. There were a seemingly limitless number of permutations. He might end up smashing his fist through the wall and breaking his knuckle like he did one night three years ago on an equally hot summer day. He might smash his knuckle because war wasn't what he intended. That's what he said to me that night, three years ago, on an equally hot summer day. We were in his apartment drinking beer and listening to Wagner on his cassette player when he said: War wasn't what I intended.

What did you intend it to be? I asked. A walk in the park?

I just didn't intend it to be what it was. I intended the army to be something else. For me it was a way out. A job. It gave my life structure and meaning. I didn't mind it. I liked the army. Army life is wonderful if you have the right temperament, and believe me I had the right temperament. But only to a certain extent. Sure, I understood that some killing would be involved, but I didn't actually believe that I'd be the one involved in the killing. He said: I didn't think I'd be the one being shot at. Sure, we trained for it. But it was never my intention to actually be involved with war. War wasn't my intention. I liked the training aspect of the military. I liked the command structure of the military. I liked what went along with it: the camaraderie, the self-discipline, the order it imposed on my life. I even liked, for the most part, the food. That's why I joined the military. Really I joined it for a salary, for something to do, and for the food. I liked military food. But then, before I knew it, there I was. I was a killing machine. They were shooting at me. I was shooting at them. Corpses all around. And I have to tell you: Once you smell a corpse you never forget it. It's a smell you never forget. But the thing that gets me even to this day is that it wasn't clear. I'm telling you the army never made it clear. They didn't make it clear. Sure we trained to fight and kill, but they never told me I'd be sent to war. For me, it was only a way out, not a path to corpses.

At that point he smashed his fist through the wall. I regret the corpses part of the military. They just didn't forewarn me adequately. He turned and smashed his fist through the wall. It wasn't like he was physically enraged. He just turned and did it. Smash. Just like that. A broken knuckle. Screaming ensued, then pathetic crying. First rational, then irrational. Meanwhile, it was hot as hell. We were drinking beer, smoking cigarettes, and there was *Die Meistersinger,* performed by Arturo Toscanini and the NBC Orchestra. I just wanted a way out. Those were the words he used and that was the music playing on his cassette player that particular night when he smashed his hand through the wall and broke a knuckle. That night, while he screamed in pain, *Die Meistersinger* echoed through my mind as he was icing his hand in a bucket of ice water. I just wanted a way out. Killing people, that's not what I intended.

So when it came time to making our pact with each other, and he said, Have you ever smelled a rotting corpse? I was careful not to respond with too much interest.

Remember three years ago you broke your hand? I thought we weren't going to talk about your war experience.

Believe me, you've never smelled anything like it in your life. It's a stink you never get out of your nose.

Then cover my back, I said. You must check in on me time to time just in case I drop dead in the middle of the night. That way you won't have to smell my corpse.

It's a deal, he said, and you check in on me.

And so it was. We made a pact and every few days or so, I would contact the Vet to see if he was still alive, or he would contact me.

I'd call him in the morning and he'd pick up the phone. Are you still alive, buddy? I'd ask over the telephone.

Yes, I'm still kicking. How about you?

I'm still at it, better than ever. Want to come down for a beer? And so he would drag himself down for a beer and we'd have a lovely day drinking and reminiscing. We'd listen to my music if we were drinking in my place, and my music was the Clash or the Ramones. Or if we were in his place, which was a dump just like mine was, we'd listen to *Madama Butterfly* by

Puccini or we'd listen to Wagner's greatest hits performed by Arturo Toscanini and the NBC Orchestra.

Run, don't walk. Run fast as hell. That's what he'd say to me as he got increasingly incoherent in the wee hours of the night or of the morning. If anyone ever starts shooting at you, don't take any risks. Run like hell.

That's what she said to me too. Run, don't hide. I remember her distinctly saying those same words to me. If he comes through the doors and you're lying in bed with me, trust me: run like hell.

That's strange, I said. Him? I asked, pointing to the picture of Matthew Gliss on her dresser that was looking down on us—a picture of the man whom I had thought, if memory serves me, was a reasonably decent guy. I seem to know this guy, I recall myself saying, and I remember him being a pretty nice guy.

How well do you know him?

Poorly, but what I do know of him is mildly positive—that is, if I'm thinking of the right guy.

Well that's him in the picture. Take a good look. If you ever see him walking through the door and you're in the sack with me, watch out. Run and hide. He has a Glock 10mm automatic and I've seen him shoot it down at the dump. The damage it did to steel was incredible.

SO I ASK MYSELF: Why would someone like him—Matthew Gliss, a stranger really, someone I vaguely remember as being a nice guy—want to kill me? And once I'm dead, I thought, that's it. No more me. Everything that I am will be gone. Suddenly I was hit by the horror of how easily vaporized we can be.

It's not as hard as you think, I once told the Vet. To be vaporized.

You're telling me? he asked with more than a little incredulity. Do you know who you're talking to here? Have you ever smelled a corpse? But this time I headed him off at the pass.

Gotta go, I told him.

Sure, now go. Go now—after dumping this crap about being vaporized upon me. Sure, I know how transient all this is. It only takes a small piece of lead travelling at a few hundred miles an hour. It's really not that complicated.

I left his apartment with those words ringing in my head. It's not really that complicated, he said. Not too complicated, just a piece of lead moving at a few hundred miles an hour. And then? Then what? Vaporized is what. Not bodily vaporized. But the life force that drives within is chased without—vaporized—and all that's left is an empty corpse. The blank vessel of the body lying there, useless. A few memories. All this effort only to leave behind a place marker in the minds of a few intimates. The memory that my mom and dad have of me. The memory that the Vet and Epstein have of me. The memory that a few other characters may have of me, including Addison. But Addison is very old right now and probably won't last much longer, so if I should die before he, what good is any memory he should retain of me? Like him, it too will be gone. Vaporized.

HE'LL SHOOT YOU if he discovers you here with me. She was serious. The thing I discovered about her was she was always deadly serious. All joking aside, she was pure business when it came to telling it like it is. He'll kill you if he finds you here. She wasn't being metaphorical. She wasn't even exaggerating. If he steps in on us, best you run, don't walk. Run like hell. He has a Glock. The damage that thing can do to steel is incredible. When she said that, I felt overwhelmingly as if I'd stepped into a hornet's nest.

What am I doing here? I'm only here because it's a hot day and I don't want to be in my apartment alone. I'm tired of swimming in the open water, my arms fatigued. Water water everywhere and not a beer to drink. My credit card's not working—can you help? So I stepped over the berm that naturally separates us. Nothing could be more simple. The safe was open. No one was looking. Cash was on the table. Who was I to say no? Who the hell was I to look a gift horse in the mouth? What's more, I saw her across the open water. I was taking water in through my mouth. Who knows how long I would last all by myself alone out in the open water? She saw me see her and the other way around. Two pieces of driftwood. What am I doing here? I asked myself as I went up those steps, the decrepit pool behind us, which in itself was a bad omen. What am I doing here? This was supposed to be easy as pie. Easy as drinking pop. Hell, I wouldn't even own a 10mm Glock even if I could.

So I asked the Vet, who had experience in these things. Out of curiosity, I asked him one day. We were sitting at Sal's drinking beers. Addison was pouring so we sat at the bar. When Addison poured we sat at the bar. When other bartenders were in service, we sat at a table, for we didn't like to be overheard by strangers. For all intents and purposes the Vet and I construed any person who tended bar at Sal's other than Addison as being a stranger. No matter how many years you worked at Sal's or how well we knew you, if you weren't

Addison, you were essentially a stranger to us. We didn't know you from Adam. If you weren't Addison, and you were tending bar, no matter how long you'd been tending bar, the fact is we didn't trust you enough to sit at the bar so that you might overhear our conversation. We were very sensitive about who did and did not overhear our conversation, which, in its way, was ridiculous, for our conversation, for the most part, at least as far as the Vet and I were concerned, was rather unimportant, not to mention inane. Nevertheless we did have our moments, our need for privacy, so if Addison wasn't tending bar, if Addison had the day off and someone else was tending bar at Sal's—no matter how well we knew that person, no matter how many years that person had been tending bar at Sal's, it didn't matter—we still construed that person as a stranger at least where the privacy of our conversations was concerned.

I don't want this stranger to listen in on our conversation, I would say if we walked into the bar and saw that Addison was having one of his rare evenings off.

Let's choose a table tonight, the Vet would say.

My thoughts exactly.

There was a small fireplace at Sal's and a piano in the corner and a jukebox that I was very devoted to, feeding countless one- and five-dollar bills into it, feeding it day and night as if it were my very own pet that needed a treat from me time to time.

The Vet and I would be sitting at the bar, and a silence would drift between us and I would say, I've got to feed my pet, which meant it was time to pump a few bucks into the jukebox, a jukebox I had come to believe was the best jukebox in any bar in the city. I was very proud of the jukebox, and I took personal pride in it. I called it *my* jukebox, and when I was feeling particularly fond of the jukebox I called it my pet. I have to go feed my pet, I would say when the silence in the bar became thick.

The Vet, of course, being who he is and having a tin ear, despised my little pet, the jukebox, and he was always trying to get Addison to remove it.

When are you going to remove this jukebox? Stupid, he would say. Stupid we should waste our time listening to the music on this jukebox.

Addison, who was older than the Vet by some decades and who himself had had a few corpses of his own in his past, having himself been a veteran of the European Convulsion, liked to treat the Vet tenderly as if he were his own slightly misdirected son.

Listen, my boy, Addison would say to the Vet, who was anything but a boy, when they play the music—enjoy it. It's here to be enjoyed. It's not here to drive you crazy. So sit back. Do yourself a favor—listen to it if you please, and if you don't please, then try to block it out. But above all, relax. We're all here to be happy.

This claptrap. Now if it was Wagner, the Vet would shoot back, rather ridiculously, perhaps I could take you up on it. If it was opera, perhaps I could take you up on it. But enjoy this claptrap? Impossible.

Your Der Meistersinger.

It's *Die Meistersinger.*

Der? Die? What's the difference? Meisterbator is more like it.

Your claptrap is more like it. And while we're at it, it's *Madama Butterfly.* I wish you would give it that respect. The beauty. And call it by its real name.

And so it went—the tedious charade that paraded itself as

conversation when we were three sheets to the wind and I was stuck with nowhere to go but home to my apartment alone.

THERE WE SAT near the fireplace because it was Addison's night off and a stranger was tending the bar. The jukebox was going, playing "I Won't Back Down" by Tom Petty, which is only one of my all-time favorite songs.

The lyrics to that song became for me during that time—the period when I was falling in love with Lucy—my modus operandi. I won't back down or, more precisely, Tom Petty's tune "I Won't Back Down" became for me my modus operandi. I don't know why these words, I won't back down, were my modus operandi during that period, but they just naturally were. They spoke to me where I live, I suppose.

For instance, when I was climbing her steps that first time and I saw the pool, which was a bad omen, and I was feeling a bit paranoid looking over my shoulder even though I couldn't explain why I should feel paranoid at such a moment, the lyrics from Petty's song drifted from I don't know where—an open window down below or something—and the words 'I won't back down,' sung in that song by Tom Petty gave me encouragement to press ahead, to follow her to her apartment, and even then it was announcing itself, though I didn't recognize it at the time, as my modus operandi.

So later when she broke out in garish laughter, I thought of this song, and remarkably I discovered within me the fortitude to grin and bear it.

One time she and I were having a fight—a rather violent fight, which, especially while I was initially falling in love with her, we seldom had—fights, that is. But during that rather violent fight, which was over something—I don't know what—she said—I think we were at Sal's or something—yes, we were at Sal's when she said:

Are you coming home with me tonight—Matthew's away—or are you just going to rot in this place and get drunk with your drinking cronies?

I didn't like the way she put that so I said, Rot!

Whereupon, surprisingly, she slapped me on my face not once but twice, once on each cheek. Slap, my head flies back in snapping pain and before I can recover, another blinding slap, this time across the front of my face, stinging my eyes, and then, before I could recover or say anything to mollify her, she was gone, collecting her things and marching out of the bar alone, slamming the door behind her. God how sexy she looked, I said to myself as I watched her storm out of the bar. The sexiest woman I have ever seen, I said to myself when she stormed out of the bar after having slapped me not once but twice painfully on the cheek and face.

Addison was running the bar, thank god, at the time, so I didn't lose face like I would have had it been one of those strangers tending the bar at Sal's. Addison merely cast a mournful look in my direction, poured a brandy, and, not saying a word, slid it down the bar towards me. Addison could be generous and understanding as hell, and that's why, when it came to who was who at that bar and why it was that bar and not any other that I chose to spend all my money at, I merely needed to point to Addison to make a point. I come here because he's like a father to me. A grandfather. I never had a grandfather, but if I ever did, Addison would be him.

The door slams. She's sexy as hell, I thought to myself. She's sexy as hell. Here, have a brandy, Addison says, trying to help me keep from losing face. Not knowing exactly what I was going to do next, I walked over to the jukebox and there, staring me in the eyes, was this song, which became my modus operandi. I ran a five-dollar bill into the jukebox and commenced playing over and over again, to the price of a five-dollar bill, Tom Petty's tune, which that evening became my beloved modus operandi, and it was that evening, her slap still stinging my eyes, when I realized definitively that (1) this relationship was about love, (2) she was sexy as hell, and (3) I would never let her leave, never, not as long as she and I live. And that was my only provision: As long as she and I live, I would not allow her to leave me ever—she being a taken woman or no.

That slap committed me to loving her in a way that nothing else has ever committed me to anything before or since in my life. I've never really been committed to anything in life before, never having had any feelings about being committed one way or another, but that night in the bar—slap slap, have a brandy—I felt something, and the only word I can describe that something with is the word 'committed.' Slapping me she told me that she felt strongly about me. If she felt strongly enough about wanting to have me around that she would slap me if I told her I wouldn't go home with her, then she was committed to me in very important ways that I was only beginning to understand.

Are you coming with me tonight, or are you just going to rot in this place and get drunk with your cronies?

I didn't like the way she put that so I said, Rot!

She didn't like the way I said 'rot,' either, apparently, so slap slap and there she goes her sweet pretty way out the door. Sexy as hell. She couldn't have declared her love for me more strongly than had she kissed me full flush on the lips for all to see, including old man Addison who, himself, is like a beloved grandfather to me. I go to him for all fatally important advice, his most important advice being that I enjoy life.

Enjoy, he would say, peering through the haze of all his years to offer me advice that only the haze of all those years could bring. Enjoy, he says, putting food in front of me. No rush to pay. Just enjoy yourself. You only have one life to live, and believe me no matter how old you live to be, it is still over too soon. The game is over way too soon.

HEAR THIS SONG? I asked the Vet, sitting there at a small table by the fireplace because a stranger was tending the bar.

Let's find a table tonight. Addison is off.

Let's. So we found our table by the fireplace.

The Vet was looking at a photograph on the wall, which was an unusual photograph of a young boy wearing knickers standing next to one of those old bikes with the huge front wheel and the tiny rear wheel. It was an ancient photo, probably more than a hundred years old.

If they ever close this place, the Vet said, I want that picture.

Other times he would say to me: Don't let them close that place without me getting my hands on that beautiful picture of the boy and his bicycle. I must have that photo someday. It makes me very happy.

Hear this song? I asked.

This claptrap, the Vet said.

Call it what you want.

I certainly won't call it Wagner or Puccini. I sure as hell won't ever mistake this claptrap for that magnificent music.

The beauty of that music, he would say, is unmistakable. But this music you have here is—well, it's stupid we spend so much of our time listening to it.

Call it what you want, but I love what it says. It's my modus operandi.

What's that? the Vet asked. It sounds like a venereal disease.

Anyway, the Glock.

10 mm automatic is what you were saying.

Yes. What can you tell me about it?

It's ultra small and concealable and it packs a punch. Simplicity. Durability. Accuracy. It's all there. You want to see one, I'll collect one for you.

How would you do that? I asked.

I have my ways, believe you me. Are you interested? Want to go plinking around with one, see how it fires?

Let me think on it.

Let nothing. We'll just do it, that's all. We'll go plinking with one. I'll find one for you so we can go plinking at the dump or something. How'll that suit you?

It'll suit me fine, I said, and with that a sad and ominous silence drifted between us. I gotta go feed my pet, I said. I'll be back.

I was feeling very something all of a sudden. I fed my money into the jukebox and I was feeling something. I was feeling sad. I was feeling very sad. I don't know why I was feeling sad all of a sudden, but I was feeling sad. So I played my modus operandi to cheer me up and walked back to the table.

I'll collect you that Glock, the Vet said. No problem. Thought they only made 9s but if you want a 10 I'll collect a 10.

I sang the refrain for him. Do I have to spell it out? I asked him, singing the refrain. This is my modus operandi.

Your venereal disease more like it, the Vet said.

My love, more like it, I told him.

Run, don't walk. And hide.

Are you trying to be mystical too? What are you trying to tell me?

What does it sound like I'm trying to tell you? Run, don't walk. And hide if anyone should start shooting at you.

Why would anyone start shooting at me? I'd ask. You planning to take potshots at me?

You never know why someone would want to take potshots at you. It's a crazy world out there, believe me. Do you know who you're talking to? But if they do take potshots at you, run, don't walk. And hide.

Then we'd go back to his place for a nightcap.

One more, he'd say, before we went our separate ways—I to my place, and he to his, directly above mine, which, by being a wreck, was hardly discernibly different from mine.

Or we can nightcap at my place, I'd suggest.

Or mine, he'd say. That way I don't have to travel home after the nightcap. I don't like to drink and climb steps.

Nor do I.

But I have the gimpy leg, remember. Do an old man a favor. My place tonight for the nightcap.

And so it was his place. Always his place for a nightcap.

Fumbling through the tapes with a lit cigarette between his lips, it was *Die Meistersinger* and if it wasn't *Die Meistersinger* it was Puccini and his *Madama Butterfly*. He came to opera late in life. The Vet, that is, not Puccini. That is, the Vet came to music late in life. I don't know about Puccini's life. Before he came to opera, the Vet never listened to music. He had a tin ear. He claimed he was tone-deaf. Didn't care for music at all. But one day he heard *Die Meistersinger* and it changed everything for him. Before he heard *Die Meistersinger* he had a tin ear and was tone-deaf, but after he heard *Die Meistersinger*—and it only took one listen—after that moment when he first heard the music of Wagner life was never the same for him. After that moment he lived for music. He lived for the opera. He seldom went to the opera but he went to the store and bought a cassette of Toscanini and the NBC Orchestra playing Wagner's greatest hits. I've heard him tell the story.

For me, music is life, he would say.

We would sit around his apartment, which was a one-bedroom dump, just like mine, which was also a one-bedroom dump, directly below his one-bedroom dump, and he would tell me: Before I discovered Wagner and Puccini music didn't exist for me. Stupid! I was so stupid! What a waste of years not listening to music. But since I discovered Wagner and Puccini it has occurred to me that music is life. Now, it turns out, I can't live without it. Stupid! What a waste. I went so long without music.

He used to tell me that when life was unbearable, which it often was, he'd listen to one or another of his cassettes. He'd listen either to *Die Meistersinger* or to *Madama Butterfly,* and no matter how terrible he'd be feeling, a weight would be lifted. If there were buildings blocking my view of the horizon, so to speak, he'd say, I'd put on a little Puccini, and suddenly the buildings would just go away and there before me was the beautiful glorious sun rising or setting on the green Elysian fields. And he used that word: 'Elysian.' The Vet was fond of odd words. He liked to pepper his speech with the occasional odd word. Don't worry. I'll collect that Glock for you. Why did he use the word 'collect'? I suppose I'll never know. It was just his way. He liked to pepper his speech now and then with the odd occasional word.

I'll put on a little Puccini and nothing but green Elysian fields and light.

He was fond of saying silly things like, If I were to die today . . . No, wait, he would say, popping one of his cassettes into the cassette player, popping open a beer, or lighting a cigarette. As long as I have this music, I won't die, for music is life. As long as I have this cigarette, I won't die, for it chases the smell of corpses away.

On the other hand, the Vet had very strict ideas about music. He condemned the music I played. That's when he exhibited, to my mind, his tin ear.

Often he'd come and drink at my place and I'd play my music, like "I Wanna Be Sedated" by the Ramones. It was only my favorite song, that's all. It was music that I lived by, is all. "I Wanna Be Sedated" is only my favorite song of all time, is all. We would sit in my apartment listening and "I Wanna Be Sedated" would come on and he would ask very politely what we were listening to.

The Ramones.

The who?

Are you hard of hearing?

No, the music's too loud. That's all.

You're tone-deaf is your problem, I'd say. I'd get up to turn it down.

Why do you waste your precious time on this junk? he would say. Stupid! he would say. It's stupid you waste your time on this junk. What this is, is just noise plain and simple.

Why don't you change over to opera? Why don't you cross over and listen to *my* music? Believe you me, you aren't doing yourself any favors listening to this claptrap.

And that's what he called it: This is claptrap.

Let me change the tape, I'd say when it came to the end.

What are you changing it to? Opera I hope.

Sorry, I'm putting on some more claptrap.

Oh no. I've got a headache. I've been listening to this claptrap all night.

Too bad. Listen some more. I'd put on a new tape. This time it was the Ramones playing "Chop Suey."

And he would say, What is this nonsense?

"Chop Suey," I'd say.

It's an insult, he'd say, to the Chinese people.

Madama Butterfly is an insult.

That's an insult to me.

Well what about all your comments against the Ramones—you calling them claptrap?

I call it as I see it. And this song here is an insult to the Chinese people.

Oh to hell with them, I would say.

That's right. To hell with them. Dismiss a whole nation. That's rich, he would say.

Chop suey isn't even a Chinese dish.

It is too.

It is not.

And so we'd go back and forth like this—drinking, talking nonsense. It was all eminently forgettable.

You know what I like about our conversations? I would tell him time to time.

What?

They're almost all eminently forgettable.

I agree, he'd say. That's why I like them too.

The Vet was fond of telling about his life, and I was fond of listening to him tell me of his life, except when he got on the topic of his war experience. Then I tried to distract him from it, for I was afraid what direction talking to him about his war experience might take. Who knows where talking to him about his war experience might lead? It could go anywhere.

For instance, when we were in his apartment getting drunk he'd get up and switch the music in his cassette from Wagner's *Die Meistersinger* to Puccini's *Madama Butterfly*.

Have another beer, he would say. I'm just changing the tape.

What are we listening to next? I'd say, knowing full well what was next, for he only owned two tapes: *Die Meistersinger* by Toscanini and the NBC Orchestra and Puccini's *Madama Butterfly* by Otto Klemperer and the Berlin Philharmonic.

Whenever he put *Madama Butterfly* in, he'd grow melancholy and whenever he'd grow melancholy his nose, which had been severely damaged by acne and a lifetime of drinking, would turn a deep shade of red. When he put *Madama Butterfly* on and the music took hold, he'd grow quiet, his bulbous nose would glow red, and his eyes would mist up and then I knew there was no averting the war stories, unless I made my escape.

Whenever his nose lit up, I would switch the subject, but it was in vain. He wanted to discuss his corpses. I, on the other hand, deeply wanted to avoid any discussion of his corpses. Who knows where talking about his dead bodies might lead?

Talking about your dead bodies could lead anywhere, I once told him during a sober moment. It was my policy to be perfectly honest with him. If I had to be brutally honest, I vowed to be brutally honest. Never go easy on this guy. He's a veteran, after all. That's what I would tell myself time to time. He's a vet—he can take the honest truth. Don't spare him the truth and if it's the brutal truth don't spare him the brutal truth.

Talking about your dead bodies could lead anywhere, I've discovered. And sometimes, I don't want to go there with you.

He would call me in the morning to see if I was still alive.

Room service. Are you still among the living?

Yes, and by the way, talking about your dead bodies can lead anywhere. Who knows what may happen once you get rolling? I don't like it.

Have you ever smelled a rotting corpse? he would ask me.

Listen—save it. I don't want to spoil my breakfast. Thanks for checking up on me. Good day.

But when *Madama Butterfly* was inserted into his cassette player there was no telling where things might go, especially if his bulbous nose lit up all red and his eyes became misty.

He loved *Madama Butterfly*—but in a weird way, not simply for the music. He was attached to the story, for the Vet had a fetish for Asian women (or, as he called them, Orientals). I love Orientals, he would say, time to time, apropos of nothing.

So what. I love "Chop Suey" by the Ramones.

No seriously, do you understand what I'm saying?

No seriously, do you understand what *I'm* saying?

He had a thing for Orientals and when he played his *Madama Butterfly* who knows where the discussion could lead with him, but almost always it led back to his corpses.

Have you ever smelled a corpse? he would ask me.

Have you? I would ask.

Yes, I have. And believe me, when you smell a rotting corpse, it is a smell you never get out of your nose. Not even the jungle can take the smell of a rotting corpse out of your nose. It's a smell that stays with you. Then he would go on about his Orientals. He developed a fetish for Orientals while banging Vietnamese prostitutes as a soldier.

THE SMELL WOULD GET into your nose after weeks of being in the jungle and there was no way of getting it out. Not even the jungle could get it out of your nose.

HE LOVED TO TALK about his Vietnamese prostitutes, who, he was able to imagine, weren't so much prostitutes but women who longed for and were nurtured by his love. He was in turn nurtured by their love. He was their prostitute and they paid him not in crass cash but in love. They were his prostitutes whom he paid for not in crass cash but in love.

You're my little prostitute, he told me he would tell them. Then he would teach them how to say that back to him. You're my little prostitute, he told me they would tell him.

THOSE DAYS OF THE VIETNAMESE PROSTITUTES were often fondly recalled in late evening/early morning drinking binges. He'd fondly recall them and I'd not so fondly sit, having been talked into a corner with no way out. You've talked me into a corner here, bud. I don't know how to get out of it.

Just listen to me, he'd say.

We'd sit at his kitchen table, a dozen or so empty beer cans on the table, an ashtray overloaded with cigarette butts, then something would happen: The night would tilt towards deep night, and the Vet would grow suddenly melancholic. His bulbous nose would grow red. It had been destroyed by long years of acne, as well as the rest of his facial and neck skin. As well as the skin on his back—for on extremely hot nights he would sit drinking beer at his table and he wouldn't wear a shirt on account of the heat and I would look at his bad skin all night long while the back door to his kitchen would be opened to the porch and hot air from the city streets would blow in upon us all night long. His skin was hideous, so scarred by acne. His whole back was pitted with acne scars. His neck was pitted with acne scars. His face was pitted with acne scars. His nose was destroyed by years of acne and drinking. First it had been destroyed by acne. Then it had been destroyed by drinking. It had become a bulbous nose that would turn red whenever he became emotional. When he put in the *Madama Butterfly* tape, for instance, his nose would turn on and his eyes would mist up. He'd do his little search through all the rubble of his apartment for an opera tape. He'd find *Madama Butterfly*, plug it in, sigh with relief as the voices took hold, and then he'd grow nostalgic and talk about all those whores of war.

The whores of war, he would say. This is a story about the whores of war. He liked to say that. The whores of war. Have you ever smelled a rotting corpse? Well, since you're disinclined to listen to me tell you about the horrors of war, let me tell you about the whores of war instead. He used that word: 'disinclined.'

I'm disinclined to tell you about the horrors of war. His nose would turn red, his eyes would mist up, and all of a sudden

Madama Butterfly would start plainting. The whores of war. I knew a few, he would say. They saved my life. I couldn't take the horrors of war, but the whores of war saved me. They were my Lotus Flowers. Have you ever smelled a corpse?

On the word 'corpse,' I would politely excuse myself, for there was no telling where things could head once he got talking about corpses.

I've had enough, I would say, what with your corpses.

Their smell never leaves you.

I've got to go. Call me in the morning.

If I die how am I to call you?

And this was a very good question. An excellent question indeed.

And I told him that. This is an excellent question you raise. See, for once you're thinking.

And it was true. Time to time the Vet was capable of making some very good observations.

You're surprisingly intelligent, I would tell him time to time, and he would wave it away with his hand.

No seriously, I would say.

But he would become irritated with me. If I'm so smart, what the hell am I doing here with you? he would ask.

Where would you rather be? I'd ask.

Sometimes I think anywhere but here. I'd even take the moon.

That night though he had a terrific point. What if he died and I died on the same night?

If he died and I died then I'd be back right where I began. I wouldn't be discovered until someone smelled my rotting corpse in the fetid air. I didn't want to die alone only to be discovered some time after the fact due to the fetid odor of a rotting corpse. I didn't want to die in such a lonesome manner. I saw immediately that additional precautions needed to be made. I could see that I'd need to take additional precautions against the possibility that both the Vet and I might die alone on the same night. I discovered I had to take extra precautions against death because living alone too long by yourself forces you to take extra precautions. There was the Vet, who called me time to time, but I started to reason: What if the Vet should die at the same time as I? Then who would be there to call me to find out if I were a corpse or not? It was very savvy of the Vet to point this out. I worried about the Vet. What with his bulbous nose and years of hard drinking and chain-smoking—lighting one off the other so he smoked upward of five packs a day—it was clear he wasn't going to live forever. If he dies and suddenly I die and we die on the same night then who will discover my corpse? I would ask myself that question: Who will discover my corpse if the Vet dies and is unable, therefore, to discover my corpse? And when no one came to mind—when I could think of no one I might rely on who could call me—I naturally thought of Epstein, who would be glad to do it because he is a mystic and this is the sort of thing mystics like Epstein like to do. Epstein will be my second, I thought. I need a second to protect me against my own death, so I got Epstein in on it. It was the only rational thing I could do.

Epstein is married, so he doesn't need me to contact him like I contact the Vet, but I live alone so I need him to contact me time to time. But because Epstein already has someone looking in after him he doesn't have the same worries I have.

If you die, I pointed out to Epstein, you will be discovered by your wife. If I die, I will die alone, and unless someone is looking in on me, who will discover me?

The Vet.

And if the Vet dies, then who?

When no answer was forthcoming, I politely mentioned that maybe he could be my second.

Maybe you can be my second, I said.

I can do that, Epstein said and he meant it and so every third morning, he calls me. He's very religious about it. He calls the same time every third day, and I've found there's no shaking him loose from his regimen.

Wake-up call, he'll say, calling me in the morning before he goes off to work. In the background I hear his wife and children eating breakfast or getting ready for the day.

Thanks, I'll tell him. By the way, I'm still alive.

Glad to hear you are. It's a beautiful morning, Epstein would say, in his lovely radiant way. Full of potential. Make the most of it.

Ciao, I would say.

Adieu, Epstein would say. We were always peppering our speech with foreign phrases, Epstein and I.

Let me tell you the vérité about the Cubs, I would say, for instance.

Or he would say to me: The gringos down at the office are running me ragged, meaning the newcomers. And so we liked to talk like this between ourselves.

He'd call in the morning to see if I was still alive. *Guten Morgen,* he would say. Are you *mort* or alive?

Captain Morgan to you, I'd say, for I'd been up the previous night getting drunk on rum with the Vet, listening to him tell me about the whores of war.

They were my Lotus Flowers, he would say.

No, wait, I gotta go.

No you wait.

No you wait.

And off I'd go to sleep the sleep of the drunk in my own apartment only to wake myself up in the middle of the night to see if I was still alive. When I opened my eyes and saw I was still alive, I closed them and went back to sleep, comforted by the thought that in the morning I'd receive a call from Epstein.

Epstein will call, I'd tell myself, drifting off to sleep. He'll call in the morning. Just you wait and see. He's very religious about this. He'll call just to check in on you and when he checks in on you it will be the beginning of a wonderful day.

The phone would ring and there was Epstein's voice. In the background I could hear the happy sounds of his wife and children.

Checking in.

I'm alive, I'd say.

Hair of the dog that bit you.

Cheers, I would say, and same to you.

And he would say to me: Cheerio, old chap, and have a marvelous day.

Meanwhile his wife and children would be making all sorts of noises in the background, oblivious to the conversation that he and I were having.

It was funny that we talked this way between ourselves in the morning, and we could talk like this all day and frankly I never understood half of what he was telling me—cheerio, old chap, and vice versa. What's worse, most of the time I didn't even understand half of what I was telling him.

Hair of the dog that bit you.

Cheers and same to you.

Cheerio, old chap, and have a marvelous day.

And so it was. He'd call me every third day. He was religious that way. After he'd call me, I'd hang up the phone and call the Vet.

Room service. Still alive?

Still kicking. You?

Yeah, I made it through the night.

So did I.

It's a marvelous day, I'd say, repeating Epstein's advice as if it were my own. Make the most of it.

Thanks for calling.

I'd hear him rummaging around for one or the other of his cassettes. I'd hear him insert his tape, then press play, and there'd be a sigh of relief. Another day, but I'm prepared for it. This music is my caffeine, he'd say. Thanks for calling.

No problem.

Then he'd say to me, in his way: Before I discovered opera life was truly untenable. That was his word: 'untenable.' It was also Matthew Gliss's word, at least as Lucy recounted it. I distinctly remember her telling me, If he catches me cheating, Matthew Gliss has told me, she said, life would become untenable for him. After his life became untenable, he said he couldn't, or at least he wouldn't, take responsibility for any actions of his that may obtain.

What could possibly obtain? I'd wonder. What could possibly happen? Surely nothing would happen. He's a nice guy, after all. That's what I would tell myself whenever I felt I needed a little moral support. What I recall of him is that he's a normal decent guy. No need to worry. None at all.

The Vet found his two cassette tapes and suddenly life was tenable. Matthew found Lucy and suddenly his life was tenable.

Epstein had his wife and two kids so his life was tenable. As far as I could see everyone's life was tenable, including my own. My life was tenable so long as I woke up kicking.

I'll get you tomorrow, the Vet would say.

Sounds good to me. And off I'd go to live my tenable life.

I HAD OTHER WAYS of keeping myself alive. For instance, I always set my alarm for 3:00 a.m., just so I could get up and make sure I was still alive. My alarm clock would go off, I'd hear it go off, and I'd feel relieved. Ah wonderful, I'm still alive, I'd say to myself. Thank the lord. I'd reset the alarm for 8:00 or 9:00 a.m., depending, and then off I'd go, back to sleep, secure in the knowledge that I had so far avoided death by dying alone in my own apartment. Death in the fetid air. Epstein will call in the morning, I would tell myself, to comfort myself as I drifted back off to sleep. And if it's not Epstein, it'll be the Vet, who's nearly just as able in this regard.

I HAD COME TO SEE all of these little checks I'd put into place to keep myself from dying unnoticed and alone as themselves the signs of bad omens. It's a bad omen, I told myself, that I wake myself every night at 3:00 a.m. to see if I'm alive or a corpse. But of course, I've been able to overleap every bad omen ever put in my path. I'm a bad omen overleaper, I once told the Vet.

We were sitting at his kitchen table for a nightcap after Sal's when he asked me, out of the blue, how I would describe myself.

Out of the blue, I said: I'm a bad omen overleaper. That's how I'd describe myself.

A what?

There's never been a bad omen I haven't been able to overleap. And believe me, I've leaped over a few.

What do you mean by that? he would ask. The thing about the Vet is, he's always asking redundant questions. I don't think the Vet asked redundant questions because he was stupid. It was just his way of communicating. One of the ways the Vet communicated was by asking stupid questions. Another way he communicated was by making fairly intelligent observations. For him, the two behaviors were indispensable. Side by side with good observations, he would pepper his conversation with redundant questions. Or the other way around. First there would be a whole slew of dumb questions, followed by, out of the blue, a truly intelligent observation.

What if we should both die on the same night? Then who would find our corpses before they rotted?

Excellent observation, I said. I'll look into that and develop a plan.

One day he asked me: What about that plan? Have you developed a plan—a just-in-case scenario? What if we both die on the same night? What's your plan for dealing with this contingency?

Epstein.

What about Epstein?

He'll call.

Whom will he call?

Me.

What about me?

What about you? I'd ask, getting irritated at one of his stupid redundant questions.

Epstein's good for you, he'd say, especially if he calls you.

But Epstein doesn't do anything for me, especially if he doesn't call me. So what I'm saying is this is a bad plan.

Excellent observation, I would say. For really, it was quite a good observation.

Well?

Well what?

Well, he said, I suppose you still have a little work to do in order to protect the two of us.

The two of us? You make it sound as if we're married.

Well we are, aren't we?

Stupid question!

What if we both die on the same night? Then who will discover our corpses before they start stinking?

That's a wonderful question, I told him, for I was overjoyed whenever signs of intelligent life emerged from behind his skull.

But then there were the stupid questions. One of his stupidest questions was: What do you mean by that? He was always asking: What do you mean by that? It drove me crazy.

You're pretty intelligent, I would say to him.

What do you mean by that?

Jesus, stop asking stupid questions.

Another way the Vet communicated was by recounting tales of his wartime experience, but when he started to talk about corpses I always did my best to divert the subject.

For instance, the Vet was quite enraptured by the music of Wagner, which invariably put him in mind of corpses, or he'd play the music of Puccini, which put him in mind of the whores of war. When we were down in my apartment listening to the Ramones he'd get angry.

What is this claptrap you're always listening to?

And I would say: It's a band called the Claptrap.

And he would say: Change to opera. Change to Puccini or Wagner. You will notice a difference in your life, believe me. You will see, like I, that music is life.

If he was cleaning his kitchen and he had a broom in his hand as was often the case when he was cleaning the kitchen, for there were always crumbs all over the place, then he'd swing the broom at me, nearly taking my head off, and he'd do this to make a point. He viewed his role in life, sometimes, as being my mentor. He was twenty-five years my senior so it was only natural he'd take himself to be my mentor. He'd take a swing at my head with the broom just to get my attention and then he'd make a proclamation: Music is life, he would say. Don't forget that—music is life. You'll see what I'm saying when you give up your claptrap.

Nonsense, I would say. Life is life. Music is music. Let's not confuse things.

You've got a lot to learn, he would say. And until you change your taste in music I fear for you.

That's a stupid thing to say, I would point out, trying my best to keep to my rule about being brutally honest. What do you know about music? You yourself told me you have a tin ear.

I thought it was tin until I discovered the real thing. Then what I realized is the problem wasn't with me—it was with all that nonsense music.

Or we'd be up in his apartment having a nightcap listening to *Die Meistersinger.* The night would tilt towards deep night, he'd start getting a tad emotional, and he'd rummage around for his *Madama Butterfly* tape. Where the hell did I put that tape? he would curse. If I lost that tape, I don't know what I'd do.

Go out and buy a new one.

Impossible. This is the tape that made me fall in love with opera. To lose it would be a blow.

You should expand your repertoire, I would tell him.

Easy for you to say. You have countless tapes because you listen to that claptrap, which is just noise really. But I'm still learning this music. I'm learning it by heart. I'm still learning *Madama Butterfly*. It is all I need right now—that and *Die Meistersinger*. These two are the only tapes I need right now. No need to get more. I'm content with these.

He'd happen upon his *Madama Butterfly* and he'd place it in his cassette player. Ah, thank God for this music, he'd say, as the first chords of the music took hold.

It didn't take but a moment and he went from being a very reasonable and likeable person to a person with a red bulbous nose whose eyes misted up on him and whenever that happened he'd begin talking about the whores of war.

Believe me when I say that not even the jungle can remove the stink of corpses. On leave I'd visit my Lotus Flowers on the outskirts of the city. They were my saviors. They lived in a lean-to hut along the river. They taught me about the pleasures of living flesh—the pleasures of my flesh. After being so long with the corpses in the field I wanted to become a corpse myself. I didn't want to go on with life. But my Lotus Flowers taught me to want life. I was grateful they could teach me about the pleasures of the living flesh. I loved my Lotus Flowers. They loved me. There was no fooling in our relationship. It was very pure and honest. You could not fool what we had—me and my Lotus Flowers.

Cornered, I tried to find an out. Look, I'd say. I've heard this story before. You need to move on. You need to invent new stories.

Easy for you to say, he'd say. You who have no stories to offer. Easy for you to say 'get a new story.' Good night, he'd say, slightly enraged. You may call me in the morning—you who have no stories. But now you must go. I don't need you now. I have my music. That's all I need is my music. Good night to you who have no stories—none at all.

IF MUSIC WAS LIFE for the Vet, life was a mystery for Epstein. Epstein was one of these people who was mystical through and through. It was Epstein's nature to be mystical. He wasn't like the Vet, who, suddenly one day, picked up opera and it changed everything. For Epstein, there was always only one path in life. It was a mystical path. A journey of a thousand miles begins with a single step. That was Confucius, who was also a mystic, and occasionally I would quote that phrase from Confucius just to please Epstein.

A journey of a thousand miles . . .

Confucius, Epstein would say before I could finish. Yes, I'm familiar with that quote.

He was a mystic too, I would say.

Too? Epstein would say, wondering, quite innocently, who the other mystic was I was referring to.

He is a mystic through and through and his wife, Meg, doesn't understand it, and I don't understand it either. He's most mystical for me when we're fishing at our favorite fishing hole on the Des Plaines River somewhere in the forest preserves. In the distance beyond the forest preserves is the traffic hum, for the forest preserves are surrounded on all four sides by highways. Small-engine planes pass overhead, flying in and out of a nearby municipal airport. But at the spot where we are fishing alongside the river, for all intents and purposes, it's a virginal wilderness.

This is a virginal wilderness, Epstein would say as we hunkered down in our spot to fish for carp.

And I would agree. For all intents and purposes it is, I would say.

No one comes into the forest part of the forest preserves, do you notice? Everyone sticks to the road. As a result, this place—these woods—are essentially untouched.

We're sitting on the muddy bank of the Des Plaines River that runs through the Cook County Forest Preserves, which is, for all intents and purposes, a virginal wilderness, like Epstein says. Across the muddy river, there's a blue heron pecking mud. Or there's an egret pecking mud. Or mallard ducks quietly swimming on the surface of the muddy river. Or from the tree branches overhead, there's a crow cawing, and if one crow is cawing then there will be more crows cawing from deeper in the woods and their caws echo the caw of the crow above us and above the blue heron that is pecking mud, and the forest of the forest preserves is a veritable forest of oak trees and maples, their branches heavy with leaves and seeds and nuts. The river is silent as it moves quietly downstream and as it moves quietly downstream it seems to silence the woods. It's a muddy river and the banks of the river are muddy, and a heron is pecking the mud with his beak and the crows are cawing and the forest preserves are, for all intents and purposes, a virginal wilderness. Epstein and I are sitting next to each other on foldout chairs, our rod holders are stuck in the muddy bank, we have bells at the tips of our rods, and the pull of the river on the lines causes the bells at the tips of our rods to jingle ever so slightly. In such conditions as these Epstein is, for me, at his most mystical. In such conditions as these, when we are out here fishing in the virginal wilderness, nothing needs to be said. When we are out here fishing in the wilderness Epstein is the most parsimonious man I know. He doesn't say anything but the most essential words and he doesn't make any but the most essential gestures or movements. In such conditions as these, which are the conditions of us fishing in what is essentially a virginal wilderness, Epstein never says a peep. Epstein can be quiet as a stone. Motionless as a stone. Out here in the virginal wilderness, Epstein is, for all intents and purposes, a stone. He becomes a stone out here. It's part of his mysticism—the core part of his mysticism. He is essentially a stone when we are fishing at our hole in the forest preserves and the rest of the world ceases to exist for him. When we are out here fishing he is no longer Epstein the man but Epstein the stone. He no longer is Epstein who has a wife and two kids who are busy getting dressed in the morning or eating their breakfast, laughing while he calls in to check and see if I'm alive or dead. Out here he is at his most mystical, which is to say, he is only Epstein the stone. He was mystical about nearly everything under the sun, except when talking about the troubles at the office. Then Epstein was harried and harassed, no different from the rest of the world. The gringos down at the office are running me ragged, he'd say. Sometimes he would simply be baffled in the face of the gringos, meaning the newcomers, whom he suspected were trying to supplant him at his office.

The gringos are trying to supplant me at the office. They are trying to take over. As a result they're running me ragged.

At times he could be rather philosophical about it, saying, I suppose if I were in their shoes, I'd do the same thing as the gringos. I'd try to supplant me too. I don't blame them, really.

But other times he was just exasperated. The damned gringos at the office are running me ragged.

On other things like fish, Epstein was a saint. He was capable of enormous mysticism and solicitude. I didn't understand half of his mysticism. Even his wife, Meg, a childhood sweetheart of his, didn't understand even the smallest bit of his mysticism.

I don't know where he gets it, she would say, baffled by his mysticism.

But there was something there, something special about our Epstein. That's what we called him, Meg and I, our Epstein. Other times I would refer to him as my Mystic. I think it's time I called my Mystic, I would say to myself, and then I would call him. If his wife answered the phone, I would say: How's our Epstein doing? And once in a while she might even say: You mean our Mystic?

He was full of a sense of oneness and he never wasted any time expressing that oneness when we were out fishing at our hole.

When we were fishing at our hole he wasn't even Epstein harried by the newcomers, whom he called gringos. He was ancient and simple as a stone.

At such moments I would get uncomfortable around him, for he had become a stone, and here I was—this person who was unable to become anything to speak of, really. I mean I had never really accomplished anything I had ever set my life to. Partly because I think things had never gone my way. Partly because in some way I too was like a stone and never set my life to anything other than sitting around. I have never really been interested in accomplishing anything and, in the end I suppose, as a result, I have never accomplished anything. I've been content, so to speak, to sit in my apartment and wile the hours away. Wile them away as if I had an infinite supply of days. And the days melted into years, and that's when I thought to myself: I best gas up my car.

So, apropos of nothing, other than a desire to get out of my hot apartment on a searingly hot day, apropos of nothing really at all, I gassed up my car.

Hot, huh?

Yes.

I suppose it'll get worse.

I suppose so.

It always gets worse before it gets better.

Isn't that the truth, I said, trying hard not to pay attention to anything in particular.

Then I thought of Epstein. He can fish by himself today, I said to myself. He can fish without me. My Mystic. Then I realized in a flash that Epstein in fact doesn't even need me. I'm not needed when we go fishing in the virginal wilderness together. Why am I needed? He only sits there and mystically transforms himself into a stone. If he can be a stone in my presence, surely he can be a stone in my absence. It was that sense that Epstein could get along without me—a realization that, by the way, tore my heart out with grief—that partly contributed to my going with her to her home that afternoon.

Run, don't walk, the Vet says.

Nonsense. Are you going to start taking potshots at me?

You never know.

But Epstein and you can get along without me. It's totally evident that this is the case.

Besides the bank vault was open and I was tired of swimming.

Epstein, I told him one day, out of the blue, I'm tired of swimming alone.

Epstein being Epstein—that is, being a mystic and having mystical insight—knew exactly what I meant.

I understand what you're saying, he told me. His understanding what I was saying was an act of tremendous solicitude.

Your understanding is a gift, I told him. Thank you for comprehending what I'm saying.

It's simple, really, he said. You're tired of swimming alone. I can see that you are. What you need is to find a beach so that you can rest.

THERE I WAS gassing up my car. I was minding my own business, really. I like to mind my own business and now I see, in many ways, Epstein has been my mentor in this matter as well. Epstein was terrific in this way, for Epstein too was always minding his own business. It was his way, in a small way, of being like a stone. In social situations he minded his own business, except, of course, when it came to the gringos. Then he'd get harried and harassed. The gringos down at the office are running me ragged, he'd say.

Or: The gringos are trying to supplant me at the office. They are trying to take over. As a result they're running me ragged.

But in all other social situations Epstein minded his own business. He never asked, for instance, about the Vet. He knew I spent enormous amounts of time with the Vet because I would tell him about it, but he never asked about the Vet. He always waited for me to tell him about the Vet.

Got drunk last night.

Oh, yes, Epstein would say, curiously, but he'd never ask who with nor would he pass any sort of judgment even though both he and I know he disapproved of my spending so much time drinking with the Vet. His inability to pass judgment in this matter even though, underneath everything, he was skeptical of most of my relationships with other people was another part of his solicitude.

I'd tell him: I got stinking drunk with the Vet. We were up in his apartment listening to some of his music. We just sat there and got drunk.

Later, after I started going out with Lucy, he never asked about her either. So, time to time, I would tell him about it.

Got drunk last night, I would say.

Oh, yes, he would say nonchalantly, not asking who with.

With this woman I've been seeing lately, Lucy.

Later I would wake up next to Lucy at her place. Matthew Gliss was out of town on a business trip. I'd wake up early in the morning out of habit on Epstein's third day wake-up calls, and I'd lie there in bed next to Lucy, wondering what Epstein thought as the phone rang unanswered in my apartment—provided he was following through on his promise and calling me.

Does he think I'm dead? I would say to myself, lying there awake in Lucy's bed, wondering. I would lie there awake next to Lucy, who was an incredibly sound sleeper. I would wonder about Epstein while Lucy slept soundly by my side. When Lucy's awake she's extremely alert but when she sleeps she sleeps the sleep of the dead and occasionally I would wake her to make sure she wasn't dead.

Lucy, wake up, I would say, rocking her gently. When she wouldn't wake up because she was such a sound sleeper, I'd shake her a little more vigorously, or I'd listen for her breath, or, sometimes, I'd put my hand on her breast, and she'd wake up, startled because my hand was on her breast.

I was checking for a heartbeat, I would say. I was afraid you might be dead.

You were checking for a heartbeat, she would say, not so innocently, and then one thing would lead to another, and I always enjoyed mornings waking up next to Lucy.

But before she woke up I would lie there awake in the morning feeling the absence of Epstein's phone call as if I'd missed some crucial thing and I'd feel inexplicably saddened by not hearing his pleasant voice or the pleasant voices of his wife and children as they went about getting ready for the day. I'd lie there awake in her bed, saddened by a strange feeling that I was missing something that could only be the sound of Epstein's voice and of his happy family. And I would lie there wondering: If he's calling me and I'm not answering, is he assuming that I'm already dead? And if he's assuming that I'm already dead, what's he doing about this assumption? Is he calling the police? 911? The fire department? Is he piling into his automobile and heading over to my house?

Knock knock. He bangs on my door.

No answer.

Knock knock.

Still no answer.

Shall I knock the door down? he wonders. *Shall I enter Robert's home forcibly? Is he dead? What should I do? Shall I call the Vet? No, I dislike the Vet. I'll leave the Vet alone. I'll leave Robert alone as well. Surely there must be some explanation why he isn't home, or if he is home, why he's not answering either his phone or the door.*

Surely there must be a reasonable explanation. Robert must be somewhere—certainly not dead. Perhaps he's found a woman and he's staying at her place. Yes, that's a better explanation than the belief that he's dead. It's a more solicitous explanation. So, for the time being, I'll believe he's not dead—and I'll believe this until proven otherwise. Surely he's alive. He must be alive somewhere, somehow. Perhaps he's with that Lucy woman. I won't call her. I don't approve of her either though I'd never tell Robert that. Now, now, I must go—forward to work and deal with all these gringos.

UNLIKE EPSTEIN, IT WASN'T TABOO for the Vet to poke his grubby bulbous nose into other people's business. It certainly wasn't taboo for him to poke his grubby bulbous nose into my business. When I told him about Lucy, he said: What did you go and do that for?

What for?

You know what for.

Because the safe was empty and nobody was looking.

Ha. Ha. That's not the reason. There's more—I know it.

Because I was tired of swimming out in the open sea by myself.

That's partly the reason but surely there must be more.

Smart observation, I pointed out.

Well, what more?

I was too much alone in my apartment. The heat.

Yes, that's it, he would say. Now we're talking. Now we're cooking with gasoline.

I was worried about being alone in the heat by myself. Alone in the fetid air. Afraid my corpse would grow fetid in the hot air. Undiscovered. Alone.

Yes, that's it, he would say. That's the ticket. Alone in the fetid air. The corpse. That's absolutely it. Have you ever smelled a corpse by the way? Never get it out of your nose. Now come, come—where did I put that tape? I must have put it somewhere. I want you to listen to this. He'd rummage around the junk in his kitchen or if he'd cleaned his kitchen but still couldn't find it he'd curse himself for ever deigning to clean his apartment in the first place.

I should have never cleaned this shit hole. Should have left it as is. But it's like a penance to me. Cleaning for me is like a penance. Sometimes, I just have to be penitent and clean. Ah here it is. Now I have it. He'd pull out his *Die Meistersinger* tape from beneath a pile of junk that he had shoved into a cabinet drawer. Ah this is it. This is what I wanted you to listen to. He'd pop it into his cassette player. Yes, let me tell you. Alone in this heat in the fetid air. This will calm what ails you.

He'd rewind his tape to a certain spot but it was the wrong certain spot so he'd fast-forward to a different certain spot and when that spot was wrong he'd rewind. Fast-forward. Rewind. Fast-forward. And so on until he found the exact certain spot he wanted me to hear—a spot, I might add, no different, at least to my tin ear, than any of the other spots on his tape.

Listen to this, Robert, my friend. Yes, this is it. This will calm what ails you, Robert. Now sit back. Listen to this. Listen to beauty.

He'd play his music. Sit back, he'd say, calmly, soothingly. This will do you a world of good, Robert. The beauty. Just go ahead. Listen to this music. Nothing like it really. And he used that word 'beauty' often when he was drunk. The beauty, he would say, apropos of nothing, often repeating it, apropos of nothing.

Here—have another drink, I'd say. He was already stinking drunk and incoherent. Conversational drift was rampant when he was drunk and following him wasn't so easy. By the end of the night he invariably reached the same verbal destination—the beauty, the beauty—and I'd inevitably arrive there with him provided I'd stayed long enough, having gotten cornered, unable to get away.

The beauty, he would say. Music is life, he would say. The beauty . . . the beauty. And occasionally he would add: Haven't forgotten about it. The Glock. I'm in the process of collecting one. Very sticky operation getting your hands on these Glocks. You say 10mm. I didn't know they made a 10mm. I thought only 9mm. But I'll get you 10mm if they make them. If that's what you want. Yes, I think a Glock 10mm would be a very nice weapon to collect. Then we'll go plinking down at the dump. I'll take you there. I'll show you how the whole damn thing works. Have you ever been to the dump plinking before?

And there I was: Before I knew it, he had me nearly cornered without a getaway. We were one conversational step away from the dreaded corpses.

Remember that time breaking your finger—punching your hand through the wall? I would tease time to time, hoping to wrangle my way out.

I forgot, he would say, rubbing his knuckle.

Well you forgot something, and what I think you forgot was that you weren't going to bring up corpses anymore.

I can't help it. It's part of my nature now. Unfortunately.

And the way he said that: It's part of my nature now. Period. Unfortunately. Period. The corpses. He was so melancholy when he said it.

It's made you melancholy—these corpses, I pointed out.

It's not what I intended to be the focus of my life. I never intended for corpses to be the focus of my life.

What did you intend to happen?

Well if I hadn't been sent over to war—if I hadn't been drafted—I had my sights on something else.

What else?

Photography.

An artiste!

I'm serious. Cut it with that shit. But, yes, an artist. It was my dream.

Then why don't you do it?

What?

Live your dream.

I do, he'd say, pointing to his famous book. There's that. That's my dream.

So together we'd sit there listening to his music, *Die Meistersinger* by Toscanini and his NBC Orchestra, or Puccini and his *Madama Butterfly,* until late in the night. Smoking. Drinking. Rewind. Fast-forward. The beauty. He'd pull out his famous picture-book album from off a shelf that was otherwise bare of books—for he wasn't a reader by any stretch of the imagination, although I secretly lived in terror of the day when, picking up a book like *The Old Man and the Sea,* he'd suddenly discover that literature too was life.

The Old Man and the Sea.

Yes.

It's life. Really, it is. Stupid. Stupid that I have gone so long without reading. What a waste.

Until that time, his shelves were bare of books; however, there was that peculiar picture book—which was a creation all his own. We called it his famous picture-book album because written on the front of the album are the words 'Famous Pictures' in his own hand and just beneath in smaller letters 'By a not-so-Famous Artiste.' He spelled it that way: 'Artiste' with an 'e.' When I saw it for the first time I laughed my ass off. The Vet an artiste—what with his *Madama Butterfly,* his whores of war, and the beauty, the beauty.

Here—have a look at some of my famous pictures, he said the first time and each subsequent time he's ever shown me the famous picture book.

An artiste, I said. He waved my comment away with his hand.

Get off that shit, would you? I'm telling you—it's driving me crazy. But yes—in some of the pictures I aim at times for an artistic effect.

I page slowly through his pictures, laughing here and there at what I see. At the extreme uniformity of what I see. At the humanlessness of what I see.

Pictures should be of people, not abandoned bicycles, I tell him.

Pictures can be whatever you want them to be, he tells me.

I suppose that's the artiste in you talking.

I said get off that shit, would you! And by the way, if they ever close down our bar, remember to help me obtain the black-and-white picture of that beautiful boy and his bicycle. That picture makes me very happy.

His famous photo album contains hundreds of pictures of abandoned bikes with missing wheels, seats, and handlebars—bikes that were abandoned but that had remained, by lock, attached to bike racks, trees, or fences.

My catalog of the damned, he called it one evening. Another evening, whilst I was haphazardly going through his picture book, he asked: You like it? All those abandoned bikes?

It's interesting. Yes, I'd say, being brutally honest. I suppose I do like some of them. But they're awfully repetitious.

Life is repetitious. Don't you see?

You're too old to give me advice.

Nonsense. You're too young not to take it. Life is repetitious. Get used to it.

And you know, he had a point.

All right, point taken.

Later while fishing with my Mystic in the virginal woods I had an opportunity to throw that one out at him. I started with Confucius: A journey of a thousand miles begins with a single step.

Yes, my Mystic would say. Confucius. I'm familiar with the quote.

So here we are again at our spot in the woods.

The virginal woods, he corrected.

The virginal woods. Thanks for taking the time to come out with me.

Nonsense. I wouldn't miss it.

And then I sprang the Vet's observation on him just to see how he'd take it. Life is repetitious, I said. Don't you see?

And he, my Mystic, said: Oh, I know. That's what I love about it. I'm not afraid of repetition. I cherish it.

With that he grew quiet, and when he grew quiet I knew he was transforming himself from a man named Epstein into a stone named Epstein, there in our spot in the wilderness, the muddy water moving quietly by, our little bells twittering at the motion of the current and two herons with their long thin beaks standing stealthily in the water pecking quickly at the mud and caw caw from the tree overhead and the echo of the crows as one and then another resound like the beat of a note through a telegraph line and the woods were virginal and the woods were mystical and out there in our spot, the sun, which, as it set, bled through the tops of the densely green trees with an intensely red red. Bloodred red—7,000 bloodred-angstroms red. And there I sat quietly next to my friend, who, alarmingly, was becoming a stone before my very eyes, becoming a stone whether I was there or not, becoming a stone for the sake of oneness with all the sacred living and nonliving creatures in that virginal space.

Life is repetitious.

Oh, I know. That's what I love about it.

Life is repetitious.

Oh, I know. That's what I love about it.

Life is repetitious.

Oh, I know. That's what I love about it.

And so went my days—one day bleeding into another bloodred day into another bloodred-7,000-angstroms day bleeding life is repetitious, oh I know that's what I love about it—and I wasn't accomplishing a damn thing with my life, really, but is that what life is all about? Is it a blood ax to wield in conquest of accomplishing things? Apparently so, I would say to myself time to time, else I wouldn't be asking such questions. Apparently not, I would say to myself time to time, else I wouldn't be living the way I live—not accomplishing a damn thing at all.

Do we, must we live to accomplish a damn thing and vice versa? I would ask myself sitting alone in my hot apartment. Is life this massive blood ax that we are given to wield if we so choose in conquest of accomplishment? And if we are given an ax whose sole purpose is to wield to be put to use then how can we in good conscience let the blood ax sit all day long in the corner collecting dust and rust? My life is a blood ax collecting dust and rust and I would say this to myself time to time in order to allow myself the opportunity to recognize the situation for what it is: My life is a blood ax collecting dust and rust. In order to recognize the full and heavy ramifications of the blood ax sitting all day long unused, leaning unused in the corner, I would periodically say to myself: Your blood ax is sitting in the corner collecting dust and rust. You need to recognize, I would tell myself time to time, that your blood ax is sitting in the corner collecting dust and rust and is that why you've been given this blood ax so that it can go on collecting dust and rust like some trophy that has yet to be awarded collects dust and rust on the shop floor? And I never had a good answer. Some days saying yes other days saying no and just as many other days undecided and so just sitting on my couch or on my chair looking out the window like an unused blood ax at the passing seasons or the passing day or the light changing from morning to noon or from dusk to dark or from dark to dawn or watching the tube and whenever I got locked into a tube-watching cycle heaven help me when I did for I did not often possess the escape velocity once locked under the spell of the tube to escape its spell and so it became a vicious take-no-prisoners tube-watching cycle that would bring me nearly to destitution not to mention self-destruction for as I watched the tube I'd get into obsessive tube-watching mode and I would lie on my couch watching the tube, endlessly flipping through the channels, watching the tube and had it been a different era I might be watching the wick of an oil lamp fueled from the lard of humpback whales and indeed I might have been better off humpbacked than an unused blood ax but no it's this era and my fixating on the pixilated tube would result in countless lifetime hours spent absorbing countless commercials for countless products I could never care to use and the dishes would pile up and all sorts of discarded refuse from carryout and beer cans and cigarette butts would pile up and mold in my coffee cups and grime in my tub and shards of soap in the soap dish and my beard hairs growing untutored and my eyes bloodshot and my soul weary from all the countless hours of tube watching for countless products I could never care to have and once I was in tube-watching mode I would occasionally hear a quiet voice say to me, It's time to get up and step outside and do something with your blood ax. But another more powerful voice told me not to move a muscle to become perfectly still—a stone—in front of the pixilated light from the tube and the first voice would be choked by the second voice and I wouldn't have the escape velocity and one day a knock and the Vet at the door and suddenly I'm shaken awake from my slumbers, the Vet knocking on my door, chasing the monster away.

Come in.

Checking in on you, that's all. Haven't heard from you lately.

Yes. Thanks for stopping in. Want a beer?

Too early for beer, big guy, but I was wondering: you game for the track?

Am I game? Bless your soul! I'd give anything to get out of this dump.

And so he and I, the Vet, were off, on our way to the track and once again I'd been rescued from my slump in front of the tube. And whenever I was rescued from my slump in front of the tube I felt grateful—grateful that I'd been rescued, for had I not been rescued there's no saying what might become of me alone in front of the tube in the hot fetid pent-up air of my apartment alone.

ON THE WAY TO THE TRACK he says to me: By the way, I collected the Glock. After the races what do you say you and I go plinking at the dump?

It's another bad omen, I say to myself, that he's collected the Glock to go plinking.

Hey, the Vet says on the ride out to the racetrack, I've collected it. You game to go plinking at the dump after the races?

And then during the races he says it again, in passing only, at the end of the fifth. We can leave now, if you want. I'm tapped out. What do you say we go plinking at the dump? I brought it with me.

What do you say, I think to myself, other than this is another bad omen? Have I stepped into a hornet's nest? I wonder. And what have I done by bringing the Vet into it?

Want to go plinking?

Have you collected the Glock?

I have. What do you say we plink around with it?

And then I think: I've overcome every other bad omen that has gotten in the way. Why not overcome this bad omen as well? So I think: Why the hell not? And I told him: Sure, why the hell not? Hmmph. Very interesting, I think to myself. I, who wouldn't own a Glock even if I could, am now headed out to the dump to go plinking with a Glock the Vet has collected.

We're at the dump plinking with the Glock.

Why do you want this thing anyway? the Vet asks.

I didn't want it. You're the one who's collected it, remember?

Oh, yes, beautiful piece of mechanicals, this gun here.

Crows sounding from the top of the dump heap. From the top of the dump is a flock of seagulls. Foxes crawling around the dump heap. All sorts of trucks in the distance crawling up and down the dump heap. The dump is a huge heap and around the perimeter of the dump are some woods. We stand in the shadows of the trees of the woods and face the dump, which rises in front of us with terrific immensity. It's an immense man-made dump. A gigantic mountain of trash. The trash heap is a huge dump and surrounding the dump are trees and from the trees are crows cawing, and in the distance at the very apex of the dump is a flock of seagulls so far from any body of water and scuttling by in the periphery is a skunk. And I stand there with the Vet while he's plinking away at the mountain of trash with his Glock, which in comparison to the mountain was truly puny. There he is with his Glock, plink plink plink. And I wouldn't own a Glock even if I could. But there I am standing next to him and all of a sudden I have an inspiring idea: Try to be like Epstein the mystic. Show the Vet what you can do in a place like this, crows overhead cawing deep into the woods. Show the Vet what Epstein would do if he were in a place like this. If Epstein were in a place like this, I tell myself, he wouldn't be plinking at the trash with a Glock. If Epstein were in a place like this he'd be treating it as if it were the most sacred place in the world, for even trash, I thought to myself, even trash is sacred to Epstein. Epstein is one of those rare humans who would be able to come out to this place and see the sheer natural beauty of it. This is beautiful, he would say, standing next to me becoming a stone. This is nearly a virginal wilderness. Don't you see? he'd say to me, and while I stand there next to the Vet who's plinking away with his Glock I want to tell him that in reality what he's doing is trying to destroy something that is virginal and beautiful.

But when I look at him, because he's having so much fun with his Glock, because he's nearly high with the fever that the power of the Glock produces in him, I keep my mouth shut. Instead I stand there and I watch him take his potshots at the dump, plinking away at random shit. Plinking away at the skunk one minute, the crow the next minute, and not hitting a damned thing.

This thing's amazing, he says to me, holding the Glock in front of him and squeezing off several rounds.

It's a piece, not a gun, pilgrim, I say in my best imitation of John Wayne.

That's right, he says. Who told you that? I didn't think you knew these things about pieces. I thought you would never know the first thing about pieces. That's why I've taken you out here to train you.

I once asked the Vet his opinion: Do we, must we live to accomplish or vice versa?

We are standing at an abandoned dump on the west side of town plinking after having left the track before the sixth race.

Only if we hope to attain immortality through our actions, he says, then plinks a few rounds. But if we don't have aspirations for immortality, then we're off the hook.

Do you have aspirations for immortality? I asked him.

Of course I do. It's only natural. Plink. Plink. We're biologically rigged to aspire to immortality. That's what God's all about—a longing not to die. Plink. Plink. Plink. But to live forever. Plink. I was never a good shot, he says, aiming at a beer can set atop a concrete block. Accuracy was my main problem in the war. Can't believe I went through that hell. Can't believe they made me go through with it. All of the killing.

And what are you doing to effect immortality? I asked him.

Showing you how to operate this gun, I suppose, he says to me, taking aim at the beer can and missing again. You see how you do it. The gun breaks down—really very easily. I wish I'd had this thing when I needed it. Now it's just good for plinking. But a beautiful piece of mechanicals nonetheless.

He says it again, breaking the gun down very slowly for me to observe and learn. Beautiful piece of mechanicals, he says breaking the gun down. Never had anything like this when I needed it. So light. So beautiful. The guns I used always jamming. Look at this. These things never jam, he says, taking it apart, putting it back together. So simple. Loading a case of rounds and unloading them into the side of a car. Plink. Plink. Plink. Plink.

I ask him again: What are you doing to effect immortality?

Nothing, he says loading another case, squeezing off a half dozen rounds, plink plink plink . . . Not a Goddamned thing and it's killing me.

AT THAT POINT the conversation drifted towards corpses. At the end of the night conversation always drifted towards corpses with expressions thrown in time to time in regards to his *Die Meistersinger* or *Madama Butterfly* as the case may be: It's beautiful. Do you hear that? Can you feel it in your heart when you hear this music—the beauty? It's the only thing keeping me going right now. The beauty of this music. It is my one and only true love. Without it I don't know how I'd be able to carry on with the smell of corpses. And once he'd mention the word 'corpses' I'd have to escape or be trapped and if I didn't escape then I'd be trapped. So without further ado I'd say adieu.

Good night, fella, I'd say. Gotta go. My pillow calls.

By the way that Glock you asked about—

Yes—

I haven't forgotten about it. I'm in the process of collecting it.

I don't know whether to say thank you or curse him. I only say good night and point out that life is repetitious.

There you go, he says, taking my lessons to heart.

IN FACT I TRIED TO TAKE most of my lessons on how to live life from Epstein, whom I admire more than any other soul on earth. I would tell him that too, time to time.

I admire the hell out of you, I would tell Epstein when we were out fishing, pulling a carp out of the river or putting a carp gently back into the river.

Nonsense, he would say, dismissively. Don't admire, he would say. Only love.

Or he might say: You believe me better, but we're all the same—we're all one. Don't you see that there is no better, just as there is no up or down, just as there is no left or right, though I heard a funny saying that two wrongs don't make a right but three lefts do! And he would laugh and I would laugh.

I love you for saying that, I would tell him.

No need getting sentimental, he would say. It's just a humorous saying.

And I would point out that I'd never met anyone like him.

I'm just a human, he would say, nonchalantly. I'm just a human.

That's what I mean. I've never met anyone like you.

Meg too was still amazed at him—at his mysticism: at how he could turn himself into a stone, for instance, or at how he loved everything under the sun—and they had been married more than a decade not to mention childhood sweethearts. She swore that her youngest, a boy, Jacob, was exactly like his father.

I swear, she would say, confiding in me when I would call up on the phone looking for Epstein. She liked to confide in me time to time, I think, because of all the people she had ever met, no one understood as well as I did or as she did just how mystical Epstein was.

Our Mystic, she would say.

Yes, our Mystic. And how is he doing?

He's just wonderful. You know living with him is like living with a guru. But our son, Jacob, I swear he's just like his father—so filled with love for all things. He even said to me the other day, he said: Mommy, when I come back to earth again in my next life I want to come back as a butterfly. OK? I mean how many kids talk like that nowadays? How many kids are concerned with how they're going to come back in their next life? Most kids his age are just concerned with being firemen or policemen.

Or train operators, I would point out, remembering back to my early childhood when I too wanted to be a train operator—wanted to be a train operator more than anything in the world.

Mamma—

Yes, Robert.

Can we ride the train today?

And so it was, one of my earliest fondest memories, riding the El with my mother the first Saturday of every month.

Do you know what day it is today, Robert? Would you like to go on a train with me?

Yes, I'd say, frantic with joy. Yes! Yes!

I UNDOUBTEDLY TOOK SOME OF MY LESSONS on how to live, I suppose, from the Vet as well. It was only natural, as much time as we spent together, that I would take the Vet's lessons to heart, but I was more inclined to consciously study Epstein's lessons and to try to take them to heart than I was to take the Vet's lessons to heart. I consciously followed Epstein's lessons but the Vet's lessons impacted me whether I liked it or not. Addison, on the other hand, who was like a grandfather to me and who had a few corpses of his own in his past, didn't have any lessons to offer, or rather I didn't look to him for life lessons because he didn't want me to use him this way. Do not study me for life lessons, Addison would say time to time when I asked him for advice. I don't want to be used this way. I'm your friend—that's all, he would say. Use me as a friend.

Addison, in contrast to Epstein and the Vet, was a loving soul—a presence of love in my life that I depended upon for reasons that I can't easily articulate.

By the way, whenever I'm at Sal's, Addison is always smiling on me, watching my progress. He'll buy me another brandy just for the hell of it. Enjoy, enjoy, he'll say. His everlasting mantra 'Enjoy, enjoy' is a mantra of joy and love.

Son, he says, time to time, enjoy! He pours me a brandy, calls me son. He pours himself a brandy. Cheers. You're making wonderful progress in life, he says to cheer me up.

Thanks, pops, for that's what I call him when we're drinking brandy together like this. He calls me son. I call him pops. He pours a brandy—one for me, one for himself—we toast, cheers, or enjoy, or he says: When it comes, the end that is, believe me when I say, it comes too soon no matter how long a life you live. But no don't let that stop you. Keep going. You're progressing beautifully in your life. I'm proud of you.

And that's what he'll say to me too: I'm proud of you. Often and apropos of nothing he has no qualms about telling me he's proud of me. He's old enough to be proud of me and to have no qualms about telling me he's proud of me. He's also old enough to tell me he loves me like a son even though he's never had a son of his own to love.

I love you like a son, Addison says to me. I'm proud of you.

Thanks, pops.

Cheers.

Enjoy.

Cheers.

Believe me when I say, it comes too soon no matter how long a life you live. Believe you me.

ADDISON'S MANTRA WAS the mantra I most enjoyed. Addison's mantra was a mantra of love and joy. Enjoy, he would say over and over again. Such a cheerful fellow, always cheerful, always on the cheerful side. Cheers, he would say, and how many times would he say 'cheers,' he being a bartender bringing cheer all day long to countless customers, raising a glass, 'cheers,' and the days bleeding into years. Cheers. It comes too soon. Cheers. No matter how long a life you live. Cheers. It comes too soon. Enjoy, enjoy. I'm proud of you, son. Cheers.

EPSTEIN'S LESSONS, though, were the lessons I most savored out of life. I wasn't afraid to use him in a life-lesson sort of way. Wasn't afraid to use him as an object lesson. I loved Epstein's whole mystical approach to life and I often tried to emulate it.

For instance, I would sit long hours on a park bench attempting to become still as a stone. I would say to myself: Now, you're going to sit here for some time and in that time you will attempt, like Epstein, to become still as a stone, to become one with the animate and inanimate in a mystical relationship to all sacred things. I would walk out to the park and find myself a park bench and when I found the exact park bench to suit my needs—there had to be the shade of trees nearby, for instance, and the smell of flowers and cut grass had to be in the air. There also had to be water nearby and preferably there needed to be the sound of a burbling fountain. When I found the exact right bench and there were a few in some of the nearby municipal parks, I'd sit on the park bench quietly and I'd have this discourse with myself: Pretend you're a stone, I would say to myself. Pretend you are a stone in this very lovely park, I would say to myself. Pretend you are a stone sitting on this bench. And I would pretend to the best of my abilities. And while I was pretending to be a stone, people would stride past on the walkway, carrying their coffee cups in one hand and briefcases or purses in the other, for people were always walking past on their way to work or if they weren't on their way to work they were walking their dogs—for the park invariably attracted huge numbers of dog walkers who were also coffee drinkers carrying their coffee in one hand, their dog leash in the other. I'd sit on my exact park bench trying to blind myself to all of this activity. Blind myself to all of these people walking by with their coffee cups in one hand and some implement like a purse or briefcase or dog leash in the other and I would sit on my bench trying to become one with the animate and inanimate in a mystical union with all sacred things. I would tell myself: Become blind to all this activity. But no matter how much I tried, no matter how much I egged myself on with a creeping sense of my own failure to emulate Epstein and to forge a mystical union with all animate and inanimate things in the universe, a sense of my own creeping failure would inevitably creep up on me. You can't do this, I would tell myself as I felt myself failing, and feel like you're going to fail at the same time. I would say to myself: How can you accomplish this mystical oneness, if while trying to accomplish this mystical oneness, you are also battling this creeping sense that you are going to fail at it? I would say to myself: Oneness requires commitment, not a divided mind. I would say to myself: You were given the blood ax to wield, not so it can collect dust and rust in the corner. Wield it! But how, I would ask myself, can I wield it if in the process of wielding it I'm afraid of wielding it?

In this way, there was always something or other that ended up distracting me from my mission of becoming a stone like Epstein on my perfect park bench and it was usually insective—a black buzzing fly for instance or perhaps a swarm of gnats would draw my attention back to the here and now, back to the park where I was sitting on my bench, surrounded by dog walkers and coffee-cup carriers, attempting to become like Epstein, one with all animate and inanimate things in a mystical union. The gnats or the flies or something else would inevitably cause me to fail despite my best efforts to emulate Epstein by becoming, like Epstein, a stone.

Like Epstein, I also did my very best to believe that every living creature was more sacred than I could ever possibly be. This included viewing every living person as if they were more sacred than I. I attempted to the best of my abilities to believe that the people in the park, for instance, the dog walkers and the coffee carriers, were more sacred than I. These, I would tell myself, are the most sacred creatures in my world. But then a creeping sense that they weren't sacred would bleed into my mind. They're not sacred, I would tell myself, and then a second voice would bleed over the first voice: They're animals. They're all noisy unpleasant animals doing their noisy unpleasant things like rushing by on the walkway carrying briefcases or purses or dog leashes and coffee cups. One voice would bleed into another and I would do my best to stop the hemorrhaging caused by these two voices. These are the most sacred creatures in the world. They're all noisy unpleasant animals doing their noisy unpleasant things. And when my mind should be most united behind my task to become a stone, it would, instead, become most divided and so I would fail, despite my best efforts, to become, like Epstein, a stone.

Like Epstein, I also tried to embrace the chaos of life and I tried to find joy even where my deepest instincts found horror and sadness. But I would invariably fail. For instance I often found horror and sadness that I lived in an era where, sitting in a public park, I was invariably surrounded by coffee carriers and dog walkers. They invariably sickened me. I was made sick by them. I often felt like screaming out at the passersby: You sicken me with your coffee cups and briefcases. Hey you, you dog walkers all, I hate the very fact of your existence.

And so, invariably, as I tried to be like Epstein, I found myself being the exact opposite of Epstein. Where he found beauty, I found ugliness. Where he found sacred humanity, I found only profane humanity. Where he found beautiful life, I only saw ugly pitiful life. I would tell myself: You can't aspire to be like Epstein, for by aspiring to be like Epstein, you only end up hating the world and thereby show to yourself how utterly small and unworthy you are to even be in the same place as Epstein.

Long periods would pass in which I would try to be exactly unlike Epstein, and when I was being exactly unlike Epstein, I found myself becoming more and more like the Vet, for the Vet's lessons invariably percolated down to me, and my life, as I lived it, more and more resembled, against my will, the Vet's life. Be careful not to be like him, I would say to myself, meaning the Vet. Be careful not to be exactly like the Vet. And the more I attempted to be unlike the Vet, the more closely I saw myself resembling him exactly.

DO YOU KNOW ANYTHING about Glocks? I ask the Vet at our place by the hearth. A stranger is working the bar.

I can collect one if that's what you're saying.

All I'm asking is what do you know about them?

Say no more. I'll collect one for you in a few weeks.

That's not what I'm saying.

Then what?

When I don't answer, he reiterates: A few weeks. Give me a few weeks, that's all. You say you want a 10mm. I thought they only made 9s. But if you want a 10, a 10 it'll be. That should be a very interesting weapon to collect.

IF YOU DIE. having run your life's course, Epstein would say to me time to time, rather philosophically, then how could you possibly ever be sad about dying when you die?

Of course, he had a point. This was his true area of expertise, knowing how not to be terrified of things like the fetid smell of a corpse, particularly when the corpse in question was one's own. But unlike Epstein, I never felt as if my life had run its own course and I was terrified of dying alone in my apartment.

Everyone dies alone, Epstein would point out.

That's true, I would agree. But I'm unable to be so brutally honest about it. I prefer to imagine I won't die alone in my apartment alone.

What's more, my life didn't seem to be running any sort of course in particular, so his 'if you die, having run your life's course' wasn't of any real value to me, for unlike Epstein who had a wife and two children, I had neither a wife nor a child and as a result I felt my life, unlike his, hadn't even begun to run its course. For better or worse my life was nearly without pattern, such as it was, even though I spent enormous amounts of my time alone in my apartment. Despite spending enormous amounts of my time alone in my apartment, I nevertheless felt as if my life were without pattern or plan. I felt as if my life were uselessly aimless. And because I felt as if my life were uselessly aimless I often found myself dwelling rather obsessively on its uselessness and aimlessness. Once in a while I dared mention this obsession to an intimate. Like Lucy, for instance.

We were in her apartment that first afternoon when I had the courage to say: I feel at times as if my life were uselessly aimless.

I told her how I felt about my life's uselessness at the time because I thought I could openly communicate to her whatever lay in my heart. I did so in the belief that it was the beginning of love—to communicate what lay in your heart to one most dear. If you want this thing between you and Lucy to be about love, I told myself, then tell her your innermost secrets. That's what I told myself that afternoon. If you want this to be about love, I told myself, then begin by communicating whatever lie in your heart to her. I lie next to her that afternoon, and when I realized that quite against reason I wanted this thing between us to be about love, I began, rather tentatively at first, to unload what was most sacred and dear to my heart out in the open for her to see.

May I confess something to you? I told her that first afternoon in her apartment in the heat. I feel at times as if my life were uselessly aimless.

We're just strangers, she said. We just met, so remember, that's why you're confessing this to me, because you think you can.

We were in her apartment, which was a wreck, and the air in her apartment was absolutely still and stifling though it wasn't fetid. Later the air in her apartment would become fetid and when it became fetid I would tell myself: This is a bad omen. Then I would ask myself: Am I stepping into a hornet's nest? However, when it came to her, during those summer weeks I invariably found it quite easy to overleap all the bad omens she had placed in front of me. When it came to her, I could leap over any omen no matter how bad it was. I remember thinking at the time in the back of my mind: There are a lot of bad omens here and, you know, it's also a bad omen that you're not taking any of these omens to heart. It's a bad omen that you're overleaping all of these bad omens in regard to her, and I would ask myself: Why are you doing this? Are you crazy? What are bad omens for, after all, but to ward off trouble when you recognize them? If a bad omen is placed in front of you, I would tell myself when I was at my apartment alone, thinking about all the bad omens that Lucy was bringing into my life, you would do well to heed all these bad omens she's bringing into your life in order to avoid the trouble that bad omens inevitably presage. However, in regard to her, I would say to myself: You aren't heeding any of the bad omens that pop up in your path. You aren't heeding them. Instead, you're ignoring them, or if you're not ignoring them, you're overleaping them. Why are you overleaping all of these bad omens? I would ask myself, sitting alone in my apartment in the heat waiting for Lucy to call. This is all terrible, I would tell myself, sitting alone by myself. All of this can lead to tragedy if you're not careful. Bad omens were put in place to avert trouble and possibly tragedy. You must heed them or, if you must, overleap them at your peril.

You're growing dependent on her, I would tell myself. That's why you're doing this. That's why you're overleaping all of these bad omens. You're overleaping all of these bad omens because you don't want to be knocked or diverted from the path, which is a path that leads inevitably to her. I would also ask myself: Doesn't the path that leads to her also lead to trouble if not tragedy? Is the path that you're following, which leads to her, also a path that leads to trouble? I would wonder. And then I would wonder: What possible trouble could there be? It's only a summer romance, is all. It's only two people tired from swimming too long out in the open water come to rest together on the beach, is all. What kind of trouble could there possibly be in something so innocent as restful love between two lovers? I would ask myself: Why not go home with her? Hell, the bank vault is open and what's more nobody is around. What could be easier? It's easy as pie. She opened the door, and I stepped in behind her. This is it, she says, though I could tell it didn't give her any pride to say so. Take me as I come. And so I took her. Garish laughter ensued but I grinned and bore it. Meanwhile that picture of Matthew Gliss stared down on us. Matthew Gliss with his beautiful smile standing next to Lucy whose smile was beautiful but not nearly as mysterious as it was in real life. And I remember thinking to myself—I remember telling myself to make a point and tell the Vet—photography can capture the beautiful smile, but it is unable to capture the mysterious smile. I made a point to tell myself as I withdrew and rolled over in bed to catch my breath. You must remember to tell the Vet, I told myself, withdrawing and rolling over to my side of the mattress, that photography can capture a beautiful smile but it can't capture a mysterious smile. It was an observation that I thought the Vet might appreciate. Be sure to tell the Vet, I told myself, withdrawing and rolling over to my side of the mattress, about how the camera can capture the beautiful but it can't capture the beautiful and the mysterious. It can also capture, of course, and catalog abandoned and derelict bikes.

We've been engaged fourteen months. I can't tell you how many years we've been together.

Have there been others? I asked her, interrupting her story and really I hated talking about this sort of thing. I hated it almost as much as I hated talking about corpses.

Asking her, Have there been any other lovers? was just as bad as asking the Vet, Have there been any other corpses?

When it came to these sorts of issues—lovers, corpses—I wanted to know as little as possible. I didn't care if the Vet had corpses in his life, and I certainly didn't care if Lucy had had other men in her life. The Vet had corpses; she had former lovers. Was there really any difference and why should I trouble myself with it? The past was the past, I would tell the Vet, and nearly every time we were together, Lucy liked to tell me about Matthew Gliss. If she wasn't talking about Matthew Gliss, then she was talking about a former lover other than Matthew Gliss, a lover, like me, whom she had dated while dating Matthew Gliss—because she had dated Matthew Gliss so long she didn't even recall how long they'd been together.

I can't tell you how many years we've been together. It seems like forever.

Have there been others?

Funny you should ask, she says. There have been seven others, she tells me. She refers to her Technicolor tattoo that scared the hell out of me when I first saw it only moments earlier, the scent of gasoline still fresh on my fingers. There have been seven others since Matthew Gliss, she says matter-of-factly. As you can see, they're all represented right there on my back.

And what does he say about this tattoo?

What can he say? He has to take me as I come or leave me.

There was the swimming pool, which was a bad omen, and the mess strewn about when she opened her door, which was also a bad omen. It's bad enough my apartment and the Vet's apartment are wrecks, but hers too, I thought, perhaps a little unfairly. It was a bad omen. But the bank vault was open, it was hot as hell, and she was easy as pie. So why the hell not?

She opened the door to her place. Would you like a cold drink?

My intention as far as I can recall was only to keep from drowning, not to fall in love, so when I stepped inside and saw what a wreck the place was, and she smiled, took off her clothes, and said, Take me as I come, I took her as she came. She pulled the shade down on that window for privacy and she stripped naked. I took her as she came and all the while there was that picture staring down at us. There was one picture in particular of the two of them standing on a boat. It's not a particularly interesting picture. But it's a picture of them in happier moments. They're standing on a boat. He's wearing a Hawaiian shirt, and she's wearing a white blouse with cutoffs, the city skyline in the background. But they look happy. At least they seem happy; they seem as if they haven't been together so long she can't even remember how long they've been together. They have these marvelous smiles—incredibly white teeth. It's the thing I most notice about that photograph: their smiles are incredibly happy. This, I said to myself, is what you must tell the Vet: Photography is about capturing the beautiful human smile of the human face, not the mysterious smile of the human face. Not the fleeting mystery of the human smile. Her lips, for she has these wonderfully full lips, seem exotic and sexy. But his lips are razor thin, and behind his smiling face, I sense tension, or rather that he's tense. Take me as I come, and there he is, trapped behind the photo frame smiling tensely at me. Garish laughter ensued but I grinned and bore it. And then, several weeks later he barges in on us—and that's when I feel it: the combination of horror (that I let myself descend this far into the abyss—a veritable well of dark longing) and terror, for I was forewarned he would kill me if he caught me and now here I was caught and about to be killed for something innocent as a summer day's sex.

This is easy as pie, I thought to myself, ignoring the omen of the derelict swimming pool, and then my mantra emanating from one of the open windows below, "I Won't Back Down," making me feel so good. Of course I can do it, I told myself, overleaping the first bad omen. Look, this is a cinch. Goodbye, first bad omen. Never been easier.

RUN, DON'T WALK. I took her as she came. The bank vault was open, the cash was on the table, and no one was looking. It was a beach that we swam to after having swum so long in the open water. We had been swimming so long, nearly drowning in the open water. That's when she saw me or I saw her and I stepped across the berm that naturally separated us and like desperate swimmers to driftwood, we clasped onto each other then swam to rest for a while on the restful beach. We fell on her bed, laughter ensued, but I grinned and bore it. And when she rolled over there was a tattoo on her back that was an elaborate tattoo of a woman bending down among seven dwarfs, though it wasn't a picture of Snow White and the Seven Dwarfs. It was only a picture of a woman bending down among seven male dwarfs. It took up most of her back. I remember feeling astonished when I saw it. I'd never seen such an elaborate tattoo in all of my life, and now, here, out of the blue—here I was with this woman. My card is not working. I stepped over the berm to help her. Would you like to come home to my place? So I followed her home. She lit her candle. We fell on the bed. Laughter ensued. I grinned and bore it and then the tattoo. What an amazing work. She was alive beneath the tattoo, but the flesh the tattoo was tattooed upon was living flesh. The living flesh upon which the tattoo was tattooed was her flesh and it was alive and the tattoo was alive. When she moved, it moved; when she breathed, it breathed. So after a moment of looking at her tattoo I couldn't tell where she ended and the tattoo began. Or where the tattoo ended and she began. They were like Siamese twins: she and the tattoo were each independent beings, but they were inextricably attached to each other. What's this? I asked.

My life, she responded.

I pointed to her tattoo. This is your life?

Take the money and run, don't walk. He'll kill you.

The tattoo that covered her back was a living being. It was attached to her as if it were a Siamese twin. The tattoo went from the scapula, marked its way along her spine and either side of her flank, branched around her torso to her belly button, and descended all the way down to the tip of her tailbone. The tattoo was a Technicolor picture of a woman who wasn't Snow White bending down among the seven dwarfs who weren't *the* seven dwarfs. Hi ho, hi ho, it's off to work I go. I rolled her over and there staring at me eye to eye was a dwarf who wasn't Dopey, and next to him was another dwarf who wasn't Sleepy, and next to him was that mean son-of-a-bitch dwarf who wasn't that mean sonofabitch dwarf who never wanted to participate in this. They're all staring at me. What's this? My life. The woman who is not Snow White bends down among the seven dwarfs who aren't *the* seven dwarfs, but conspicuously absent from the scene is the prince and suddenly I so much wanted to be the prince. I wanted to be her prince and not her dwarf. I wanted to be the one who was her prince coming to save her, not one of her dwarfs towards whom the woman who was not Snow White was bending. I don't know why I wanted to be her prince, but I knew I didn't want to be one of these little non-seven-dwarf dwarfs. To be one of seven dwarfs and not even one of *the* seven dwarfs seemed an ignominious fate. I didn't want to be one of her conquests. The bank vault was open. I stepped inside the vault and looked around. It seemed so easy. No cameras, no guards, far as I could tell, but then all of a sudden there are these seven dwarfs, and suddenly I'm having a hard time taking her as she comes because of these dwarfs who remind me of Dopey and Sleepy but who aren't Dopey and Sleepy, only former conquests of hers. She positions herself on top of me, and that's when I see Prince Charming in his picture staring down at me. He's imprisoned behind his glass. It's he, not she, who's in a glass coffin. Kiss the frog, I think, as she goes down, and after she's been down there a while, I hear that tune "I Won't Back Down." I keep saying, I won't back down. Garish laughter ensues. I grin and bear it, but how do I compete, with Matthew Gliss smiling down on me? He's the prince in the glass coffin. I remember he was a nice guy, but suddenly my mind goes blank. I no longer remember how I know him, and as I distract myself from trying to remember how I know him I in fact forget about him. That's when I won't back down, and complete disappointment is averted. I withdraw and roll over. She gets up and opens the shade.

Hot, huh?

Yes.

I suppose it'll get worse.

I suppose so.

It always gets worse before it gets better.

Isn't that the truth, I said, trying hard not to pay attention to anything in particular.

That's when I feel it. The mystery of life even without Epstein by my side. Epstein is a mystic, I say to myself, as she nudges the fan to life with her toe. Epstein knows things that strictly rational people will never know. How did Epstein become so mystical? Epstein who grew up in a working-class home and went to public schools. Epstein, Epstein, Epstein, how do you do it? When we fish together it's a holy experience. Without Epstein the world always seems dull and unhappy. But now with Lucy by my side I have that same experience, though Lucy isn't a mystic. With Lucy by my side I become the mystic. She turns the fan on with her toe. She lights her cigarette and begins telling me the story.

We've been engaged fourteen months though we've been together I don't know how long but I refuse to marry him. I just torture him a little. I just torture him till he begs me to stop. I'll just make him beg me to stop. I'll just torture him a little bit until he stops. He asks me, When are we going to get married? I don't have the courage to set a date. It's my little way of torturing him a little until he stops.

One more, I say, and so we light one more.

And then you must go, OK? she says, taking the cigarette from me and smoking it, then handing it back. We're running out of time here, she says. I'm afraid Matthew may walk through the door any moment, and if he walks through the door and finds you here, do me a favor—do yourself a favor!—run, don't walk. Get out as fast as possible and don't turn back. He has a Glock. The damage that thing can do is terrifying. He tells me if I leave him—if he catches me cheating, he has told me—life would become untenable for him. After his life becomes untenable, he says he can't, or at least he won't, take responsibility for any actions of his that may obtain.

The fan blows hot air across our foreshortened or elongated torsos.

I take this as meaning, I say, Matthew'll kill me if he catches me. Is that what you're trying to tell me? I ask her.

All I'm saying is what he told me. He tells me he can't be held responsible for anything that may obtain.

But that's ridiculous, I point out. It's totally irrational. Of course he can be held responsible for his actions—that's what courts of law are for.

Be sure to mention that to Matthew, she says, laughing as if I were the funniest thing she's ever met, when he's pointing that Glock at you. I've seen the damage that thing can do. Believe me, you don't want to be on the receiving end of its business. What's more, you don't want to be on the receiving end of Matthew's business.

Impossible, I say. I've met him. I know him, I tell her. And he's always been very nice to me.

How well do you know him? she asks.

Well enough to buy him a beer should I see him.

Then you don't know him at all. Believe me. If you knew him, you wouldn't be buying him beers. No one who knows Matthew Gliss buys him beers.

When the silence drifts between us I feel the need to fill the conversational void. So I tell her one of my innermost concerns.

Can I be perfectly honest with you?

I'd kill you if you weren't.

It was funny when she said that. So I laughed. The violence of it made me laugh. But it was probably true. She probably would kill me if I didn't tell her the truth. I came later to see that if Lucy said something—no matter how trivial—she was always willing to back it up. When push came to shove she never had any problem backing up in deed what she had only previously threatened in word.

Can I be perfectly honest?

Do you want me to kill you?

Not particularly.

Then be perfectly honest.

I feel at times as if my life were uselessly aimless.

She spoke up: Then get a job. Is that what you mean?

No. That's not what I mean.

Then what do you mean?

I'll try to explain. But when I didn't know how to explain I just let the moment pass and that's when she says: We're just strangers. We just met. So remember, that's why you're confessing this to me, because you think you can, not because you have any right to do so.

I get up to leave because the cigarette is out.

Well? I say.

I'll call.

That's it? My fingers still smell like gasoline. Any reason why I should believe you'll call me?

Oh please, don't go getting paranoid on me. I had a lot of fun this afternoon. I'd love for us to do it again.

I'm dressed, but she's naked, and that mysterious smile suddenly, briefly manifests itself, making me proud as hell.

I'll call, she says again, reassuringly.

OK, now. I say.

OK, now, she repeats. She gives me a hug. Where are you from? Idaho?

Where are you from? I ask. The enchanted forest?

I suppose.

I suppose.

OK, now.

OK, now.

Call.

I will.

I'M AT HOME WAITING at the bottom of the well for her to call. Who knows how long I'm at home waiting at the bottom of the well for her to call? It's unknowable to know how long I've been splashing at the bottom of the well waiting for her to call but I've been waiting an interminable amount of time.

You've been waiting forever, I tell myself, swimming at the bottom of the well. How much longer do you think you can go on swimming? It's a good question, and someone's got to ask it, so I volunteer to ask it sitting at the bottom of the well: How much longer do you think you can hold on swimming at the bottom of the well for her to call? How much longer?

The well is certainly a lot deeper than I thought it would be, I suppose. At first I thought going home to my apartment alone would be easy. This will be no problem. I'll just go home, I told myself. I knew I had a wishing well in my apartment so the thing is should I go to Sal's or should I go home to my wishing well? I decided to go home to the wishing well instead of going to Sal's because I wanted to retain some sense of the sacred feeling I felt while I was with her. What's more there's always that chance, if I go to Sal's, that a stranger may be tending bar and this, going to Sal's only to be served by a stranger, not to be served by Addison, would be a terrible mistake. It would sully the sacred feeling I had. I decided to go back to my home in an attempt to remain unstained and inviolate. When I left Lucy's apartment that song drifted into my mind, my modus operandi, "I Won't Back Down," and indeed I won't back down. I thought to myself: I'll go home and wait for her call.

As I walked past the abandoned swimming pool, I knew I was walking past a bad omen. It was only a swimming pool, but the fact of its derelictness was a bad omen. As I walked past it I heard my modus operandi and I realized I could easily overleap the bad omen part of the swimming pool, which is what I immediately did. I overleaped the bad omen part so when I drove past the pool on my way out I only saw the swimming pool that, instead of being filled with water, was an empty swimming pool. I got into my AMC Hornet, turned the ignition, and as I idled slowly out of her complex's parking lot past the swimming pool I was reminded of the fact that I have my own wishing well at home. No need to go to Sal's, I thought. I've got my own wishing well at home. I'll go there and stay in my wishing well a while. It was blazing hot in my AMC Hornet and all windows were opened and as I drove down all the roads that led to my apartment I consoled myself with the thought of my wishing well at home. There's a wishing well in my apartment at home, I told myself, trying to console myself until I next received her phone call. I'll merely throw myself into the wishing well and see what happens. What could possibly go wrong? I wondered. I'll throw myself into the wishing well and swim at the bottom of the well until she calls. So, I go home, and locking the door behind me, I do what I say and I throw myself into the wishing well. I wish, after I had done so, that I had never gotten the idea to throw myself into the wishing well of my apartment. For one thing, the wishing well is considerably deeper than I thought. For another, while I sit splashing at the bottom of the wishing well waiting for her call I don't know how to pull myself out of the wishing well except by waiting for her call so I continue to swim at the bottom of my wishing well waiting for her to call.

When she calls you'll be able to get out of this mess you've gotten yourself into. That's what I tell myself, swimming at the bottom of the wishing well.

While I swim at the bottom of the wishing well I realize I had never imagined that the wishing well in my apartment would be so bottomless. Water water everywhere, I say to myself, remembering a line from Coleridge. The wishing well in my apartment, which I thought to be quite shallow, turns out to be in fact quite fathomless and boundless.

It is both fathomless and boundless, I tell myself, swimming alone at the bottom of the wishing well in my apartment.

How many times had the Vet come down to my apartment and there we are listening to the Ramones when he asks me apropos of nothing:

How deep do you think that wishing well of yours is?

I think it's probably quite shallow, I remember telling him time to time. What's more, I would point out, it's circumscribed by the diameter of the well.

Time to time I would tell him, apropos of nothing: The wishing well that's in my apartment is in fact extremely shallow, not to mention narrowly circumscribed, believe me.

Whereupon the Vet would attempt to be brutally honest with me. I'm sorry, he would say, trying to be politely brutally honest, but I disagree with you.

What do you know? I would ask.

I know a thing or two, he would say, insulted. You forget sometimes who you're talking to.

You forget, I would point out, it's my wishing well. I should know how deep and bounded it is.

But have you ever actually jumped into it? he would ask, quite reasonably.

No, I would say. That's a good observation. I've never jumped into it.

Then how could you possibly know that your wishing well is as *extremely shallow* and *narrowly bounded* as you say? How do you know it's not, to the contrary, fathomless and boundless?

It can't possibly be fathomless, I would tell him time to time, listening to the Ramones. I have no wishes that I can name so how can it possibly be fathomless? What's more, it can't possibly be boundless either.

How do you figure? he would ask.

So I would tell him what lies most sacredly in my heart to prove my point: Can I be perfectly honest with you? I would ask the Vet, and like Lucy he has the exact same response: Do you want me to kill you?

Not particularly.

Then be perfectly honest.

I feel at times as if my life were uselessly aimless, I would reason with the Vet. Therefore the wishing well in my apartment can't possibly be fathomless or boundless. I have no wishes.

Time will show that I am right, the Vet would say.

I hope not.

I am right in this as I am right with music.

You have a tin ear, don't forget.

And you—your claptrap is nothing other than noise!

SO HERE I AM SWIMMING at the bottom of the wishing well in my apartment and it is, contrary to my expectations, both fathomless and boundless as the Vet suggested it would be. As I swim in the boundless fathomless waters of my wishing well, I make a vow to tell the Vet that he was correct—that my wishing well, contrary to my expectations, was both fathomless and boundless.

Your well may very well be bottomless, he liked to say, time to time. Not to mention fathomless. Look before you jump into it.

Nonsense, I would say. Impossible it should be unfathomable and boundless.

Don't be so sure.

That day, I drove home down all the roads that led to my apartment. Forget Sal's, I told myself, as I drove home that day. There may even be a stranger tending bar at Sal's, and then what? What if, instead of Addison tending bar, there's a stranger tending bar? Everything would be ruined. What you need to do, I told myself, is to go home where you can remain inviolate and sacred while waiting for her call. So I went home, I closed the door behind me, and without thinking twice about what I was doing, without doing as the Vet advised, I leaped without looking into the wishing well in my apartment and I fell deep into the fathomless boundless well, falling so long who knows how long I fell into the fathomless bottom of my wishing well until I made a splash and water water everywhere.

You can leap into a shallow well like mine, I liked to inform the Vet time to time, and make quite a splash.

And he liked to point out in a way that made me think he was only being a contrarian: Au contraire, he would say. If you jump into your wishing well—if your back is up against the wall and one day you should happen to jump into your wishing well—watch out. It may very well be a bottomless boundless well.

I thought he was merely being a contrarian, but what I discovered was that he was, in point of fact, absolutely correct. He was right. I was wrong. Without taking the Vet's advice, which would have been the correct advice to take, I took my own advice and took a running leap into my wishing well, and I fell so far so deep there was no telling how deep and far I fell until I splashed and water water everywhere. And the thing is, had it not been for Lucy, there might not have even been a wishing well in my apartment in the first place.

If anything is going to make my wishing well fathomless it's Lucy, I told myself. She'll be the one who makes my wishing well fathomless.

What is this claptrap anyway? the Vet liked to say whenever I had him over to my apartment to listen to the Ramones.

And I'd say: This claptrap is "The KKK Took My Baby Away."

It's an insult, he'd say, to the KKK.

Madama Butterfly is an insult, I would say, trying to be brutally honest, to your so-called Orientals.

That's an insult to me.

Well what about all your comments against the Ramones—you calling them claptrap?

Because that's what they are—claptrap.

You talk a bunch of rot.

You talk a bunch of rot.

You have a greater ability to talk a bunch of rot than I do.

Baloney. You are the greatest rot talker I've ever seen.

Prove it.

Jump into your well someday. You'll see what I'm talking about. I'm as right about the well as I am about your music. It's rot to say your wishing well is shallow just like it's rot to say your claptrap is music.

It's rot to say it's bottomless and boundless.

If you should ever have your back up against the wall and you should want to jump into your wishing well I advise you to take me seriously. Look before you leap.

But it was love that made me leap without looking. Is that what this is all about? I remember asking myself as I fell deep into the bottomless wishing well that was in my apartment. Is that why I leaped into my wishing well without looking before I leaped—because I wanted to impress her with my feelings of love for her?

It was blazing hot. I was driving in my AMC Hornet, all windows were opened. All roads led back home to my apartment, not Sal's. If you want to impress her, I thought to myself, go home to your apartment, jump into your wishing well, and wait there until she calls.

It became clear to me as I fell into the dark space of my bottomless wishing well that the only way to deal with Lucy from this point on was in absolutes. No half measures. It was clear to me that Lucy was a woman who would never abide half measures.

Don't do anything fifty-fifty with me, she said to my back as I was walking down the steps leaving her place.

What's that? I asked, turning to look up at her, and for a moment, I was proud as hell because I saw that mysterious smile of hers, which flashed at me soft and quick.

Don't do anything fifty-fifty with me and I assure you I will keep coming back to you.

What about Matthew Gliss? I asked, trying to reflect her smile back at her with one of my own.

We'll just have to be careful, that's all, she said.

Careful?

Yes, for if he catches us, there's no telling what might happen. Anything might happen. He himself told me that if he ever catches me with another man, his life would become untenable and if it became untenable, he couldn't be held responsible for what may obtain. So no half measures. If he ever walks in on us, do us all a favor: Run, don't walk, and hide.

A friend has been telling me the same thing lately, I tell her. He's always telling me to run and I always say to him: Why? Are you going to start taking potshots at me? And he always says: You never can be too sure.

Yes, she says. You can never be too sure who's going to take potshots at you for sure. In this day and age you can't be too sure. He has a 10mm Glock that he would not be afraid to use should he catch you with me. And then, as an aside, she flashes her mysterious smile, which is soft and quick. I hope you don't mind me bringing you into this mess but when I saw you at the gas station today I couldn't resist.

And the smile, her mysterious smile, as far as I can recollect, is never mysterious in the photographs.

There were times I would say to the Vet while listening to his music: Pictures are permanent, but mystery is fleeting. Something permanent like pictures may be able to capture a fleeting image, but they'll never be able to capture the mystery of a fleeting image—like the mystery of a fleeting sunset, which once it's gone is gone forever. Like the mystery of a fleeting smile, which once it's gone is gone forever.

Nonsense, the Vet says. I don't buy a word of it.

And so her mysterious smile is fleeting yet unrenderable in pictures.

That's just not true, he says again, lighting one cigarette off the other in the heat of his kitchen.

You have a beautiful smile, I tell her while she's on top. Behind her are the pictures staring down on us of Matthew Gliss, who has a beautiful smile but not a mysterious smile. Just like Lucy's smile in all of the photographs is beautiful but not mysterious.

I'm glad you like it, she says.

It's mysterious.

Pshaw, she says.

Pshaw back, I say.

Garish laughter ensues.

I grin and bear it, withdraw, and roll over on my side. Make sure, I tell myself as I recover my breath, to tell the Vet how her smile, mysterious and fleeting, is not captured in the photos of her and Matthew.

Let me tell you something, I later tell the Vet. We're sitting in his apartment having our nightcap, *Die Meistersinger* is playing, and we're having a nightcap in his place mostly because of his bum leg, which is what he'll tell you. Let's go to my place tonight for our nightcap—then, pointing downward—my bum leg. But he and I both know the nightcaps are always at his apartment not due to his bum leg but because without his music he's conversationally useless.

If we're not listening to *Die Meistersinger* or *Madama Butterfly*, I tell him, then it seems like you have nothing to say.

What can I say? he says.

Forget about it, I say. Already we sound like an old married couple. We'll just go up to your place for a nightcap.

Fine by me.

I'm sure it is.

I'm thumbing through his famous photo album—which, the more I look at it, the more I realize that there's something to it. There's something to his pictures of abandoned bicycles, though what that something is, I cannot say.

You know what I noticed that will strike you as interesting? I tell him.

Go easy on me, he says, meaning don't be too hard on his artwork.

No, it's not about these pictures of your bikes, which I'm beginning to like. It's about pictures in general. You see, I've noticed that the pictures of her on her dresser and in her bookcase where she's standing with Matthew Gliss capture her human smile, but they fail entirely to capture her mysterious and fleeting smile that only darkness, night, and the intimacy of bed reveal.

I disagree with you, he says, being brutally honest. A smile is just a smile, he says. There's nothing more to it than that.

Oh but there is, I tell him. And then I say: You have a beautiful smile. Amazingly, he blushes.

Cut it out with that shit. Only beautiful to my music or my artwork. Leave me out of it.

You have a beautiful smile, I remember telling her, swimming for my life at the bottom of my wishing well, looking up at her standing at the top of the stairs leading to her apartment.

If the risk is too great, you can always back down, she tells me.

No, I say. Then there's that mysterious smile of hers that photos fail to capture. She flashes it and while she flashes it I'm pushed into saying: Of course I won't back down. Not after this afternoon. I promise.

Good, she says, her mysterious smile flashing. Because I had a lovely time here today and I would love for you to come back. Who knows, she adds, no doubt to make me happy, where this may lead?

Who knows? I say parroting her, for in the face of that mysterious smile of hers I don't know how to do anything other than parrot her.

Suddenly I wished I had a photo of her smile, so I could observe carefully without also having to confront the power, which is a blinding power—the power of her mysterious smile.

If it gets to be too much, she tells me, you can always move on. If the risk becomes too much for you to bear, you can always move on. There have been others, she observes.

You don't need to tell me about them, I tell her.

Please, she says. You need to know.

But I don't, I tell her.

There have been others and the risk was too much so they have moved on, unscathed. If you want to deal with me, you also have to deal with the risk that comes along with dealing with me. If this gets to be too much for you—if you don't like the risks involved—then don't come back.

She stands at the top of the stairs while I'm at the bottom of my well swimming, water water everywhere. She tells me: If you don't like risk, then don't come back. But if you can handle a little risk, if you're not afraid of Matthew Gliss and his 10mm Glock and his rage, which he says he's not accountable for, then I'd love to see you again. Don't you see, she says, flashing her mysterious smile for me to see, I had a lovely time here today.

So did I, I say. I had a lovely time. That's when my modus operandi kicks in—"I Won't Back Down"—and I tell her quite against my will, for there's that mysterious smile of hers that suddenly blindly forces me to say: No, don't worry about the risk—about me not handling the risk. I won't back down, I promise you. What's more, why should I be afraid of Matthew Gliss? He seems like a decent guy.

You know him? she asks, incredulously.

Of course I know him.

How well do you know him?

Only vaguely, but he seems like a nice guy.

Then you don't know him at all, she says, do you?

Well enough to buy him beers, I say.

No one who knows Matthew Gliss buys him beers. She laughs.

But he slaps me on the back every time I see him or I slap him on the back every time I see him.

You don't know Matthew Gliss but look at his picture and memorize his face, for should he walk in on us be sure to run—don't walk—because there's no telling what he may do.

I won't back down, I tell her. I have nothing much to lose.

No, I suppose not, she says, smiling down at me while I swim at the bottom of my well—water water everywhere and not a beer to drink. Nor do I, she adds. With that she says: I'll call, which reassures me.

I won't back down.

I had a lovely time here.

OK, now, I say.

OK, now, she repeats and it echoes all the way down to the bottom of my well—like birdsong through the forest. OK, now. OK, now. OK, now. OK, now. OK, now. OK, now. OK, now. OK, now. OK, now. OK, now.

She gives me a hug. Where are you from anyway? she asks. Idaho?

Where are you from anyway? I ask. The enchanted forest?

I suppose.

I suppose.

OK, now.

OK, now.

Call.

I'll call.

SO I WENT HOME determined not to take any half measures with her. With this woman, with her mysterious smile, I say to myself: It's clear you best not take any half measures. If you want to hold on to her, pull out all the stops.

Where've you been? the Vet asks seeing me walk up the stairs to my apartment. I thought you said you were only going to gas up your car and then you'd be right back. Instead you've been gone several hours.

That's when I first tell him about Lucy.

What did you go and do that for?

What for?

You know what for.

Because the safe was empty and nobody was looking.

Ha. Ha. That's not the reason. There's more to it—there must be.

Because I was tired of swimming out in the open sea by myself alone.

That's partly the reason, I'll grant you that. But surely there must be more.

Smart observation, I pointed out.

Well, what more?

I was too much alone in my apartment. The heat.

Yes, that's it, he said. That's the ticket. Now we're talking. Now we're cooking with gasoline.

I was worried about being alone in the heat by myself. Alone in the fetid air. Afraid my corpse would grow fetid in the hot air. Undiscovered. Alone.

Yes, that's it, he said. Alone in the fetid air. The corpse. That's absolutely it. Have you ever smelled a corpse by the way? Never get it out of your nose.

Remember what I told you about corpses.

Only asking because you were gone so long I was afraid you'd become one.

Over my dead body.

Game for drinks at Sal's?

Not today, I told him. Not after my little adventure, I told him. Thanks, I said. I want to be alone right now.

Call you in the morning?

Sure thing.

I opened the door to my apartment, slammed it behind me, and took a running leap for my wishing well and while I fell into the bottomless well I asked myself: How long has my wishing well been sitting in my apartment staring me in the eye willing me to leap into it and always I've had the willpower not to? I've always been inviolate about jumping into my wishing well. Don't sully yourself yet, I liked to say to myself time to time, by jumping into your pristine wishing well. Let your wishing well remain pristine for the time being. Wait until your back is up against the wall, as the Vet recommends, then leap. For many years letting my wishing well remain pristine while my blood ax collected dust and rust in the corner seemed like the most sensible thing in the world to do, so sensible it freed me up to do as I pleased and the days melted into years—and it went on like this for many years—me puttering around my apartment with nothing much to do, the wishing well staring me in the eye willing me to leap but me refusing to do so, lying around on the couch resting or being caught in a vicious tube-watching cycle and whenever I was caught in a vicious tube-watching cycle I knew that anything could happen. While I sat there on my couch watching countless ads for things I could never possibly desire I knew the worst that could happen would happen. When I got caught in a vicious tube-watching cycle I would neglect everything including myself, mesmerized by the pixilated screen and the quiet voice saying to me: It's time to get up and step outside and do something with your blood ax. The wishing well staring me in the eye willing me to jump, but another more powerful voice told me not to move a muscle, to become perfectly still in front of the pixilated light from the tube and I wouldn't leap, wanting to leave my wishing well inviolate for a time. My back was up against the wall, the blood ax collecting dust and rust and the first voice would be choked by the second and I wouldn't have the escape velocity until a knock and the Vet at the door and suddenly I'm shaken awake from my slumbers, the Vet knocking on my door, chasing the monster away.

I was wondering: you game for the track?

Am I game? Bless your soul! I'd give anything to get out of this dump.

And so he and I, the Vet, were off, on our way to the track and once again I'd been rescued from my slump in my dump in front of the tube.

I COLLECTED WHAT YOU asked for, he says on the way to the track. How about we go plinking after the fifth? he asks.

How about it?

Don't see why not.

And after the fifth, after we lose everything we came with, he says, Come on; let's get out of here. Let's leave while we're ahead, do some plinking at the dump. I want to show you this thing I collected. Beautiful piece of mechanicals, really. Just wait till you see how it fires.

BUT NOW I'M AT THE BOTTOM of my well swimming. I'm slightly over my head and my arms are exhausted. Water water everywhere. And why, I ask myself, swimming at the bottom of my wishing well waiting for her call did I jump into the wishing well without first checking its depth?

It should be a big splash, I thought, flying through the air, for it is shallow but as I fell through the air I realized I'd miscalculated. How many years had I lived in my apartment with this wishing well staring me in the eye and during all those years I had never attempted to plumb it, assuming all along it was shallow because my life was useless and aimless—the blood ax collecting dust and rust in the corner—and now the well is much deeper than I thought. The well is at least as deep as the Vet suggested—it's fathomless if not boundless.

There at the bottom of the well, swimming for what seems my life I tell myself: The reason why I'm swimming is because of her. She's the reason I'm swimming like this—water water everywhere and not a beer to drink. Do nothing in half measures with her, I tell myself as I descend the stairs from her place to the parking lot. Nothing but absolutes with her. What'd you go and do that for? The heat? Wrong. Alone in my apartment alone? That's it! Now we're cooking with gasoline. I slam the door behind me and run, diving headfirst into my wishing well.

Had I not seen her at the gas station I might not right now be falling then swimming into the fathomless depths of my wishing well. It is hell in the well of my apartment and I keep on falling then swimming. I was once inviolate, I remind myself as I fall into the black space of my wishing well then splash and swim for the life of me. How much longer can I keep this up? I ask myself, swimming in the fathomless well. Long enough for the phone to ring I hope, I said. I hope I can continue to tread water until the phone rings, rescuing me from my wishing well. I was once sacred and inviolate alone in my apartment and then I found her and it made me wish to jump into my wishing well and now I've done it—I've jumped without looking into the wishing well that sat inviolate so many years in my apartment alone staring me in the eye willing me to jump.

There I was sitting on my couch in a vicious tube-watching cycle, my blood ax collecting dust and rust in the corner when the wishing well that took up so much room in my apartment would raise its terrible head and dare me to jump.

You're a very shallow well, I liked to tell it time to time. You're not a deep well at all. Impossible you should be anything but shallow, for I have no wishes at all. My life is uselessly aimless.

Then jump, the wishing well would say. If I'm so shallow, then jump.

I'm not going to be tempted, I would tell the wishing well time to time. You may tempt others with your terrible eye but you're not going to tempt me.

But my back was up against the wall, and I did as the Vet suggested.

Don't jump into this wishing well in your apartment until your back is up against the wall. When you jump, though, be sure to look before you jump. There's no telling how deep or boundless this well is.

I jump without looking and now I'm swimming out in the open water alone, swimming so my arms are tired from exhaustion. Who knows how long I'm out there swimming alone when I see in the distance a beach to rest upon. As I swim towards it, the stars overhead lighting my passageway, I remind myself that the last beach I swam to, having swum alone in the open water so long I could no longer go on, was with her.

My credit card's not working.

We float towards each other like two pieces of driftwood encountering each other in the open ocean.

It's not? I say. Let me help you with that. I step across the berm that naturally separates us and before we know it we wash up on the restful beach of her bed.

Why'd you do it? Epstein asked.

For rest, I tell him. I was tired of swimming alone. We needed a restful beach to rest upon.

I understand that, he said. And I remember—as he said, I understand that—thinking to myself: The reason why I love Epstein more than any other soul on earth is because his understanding is enormously solicitous. It is pure and generous.

Do you have any idea, I would tell Epstein, my Mystic, time to time, how enormously solicitous you are? You are the most generous person on earth.

Give to get, Epstein would say in the most abbreviated fashion. You want? Then you must give. It is so simple.

Simple in theory, but in practice so difficult.

But the rewards, Epstein would say. The rewards for giving first are so very much worth it, believe me.

When I hung up the phone with Epstein—after calling me in the morning to see if I was still alive—I called the Vet to find out if he was still alive. I'd go from talking to Epstein on the phone, his happy wife and children making happy sounds in the background as they went about getting ready for the day, to talking to the Vet who lived above me in a dump very much like my own one-bedroom apartment, which was also a dump. I'd go from talking to my Mystic, whom I admired more than any person in the world, to the Vet, whom I was probably more alike than any other person in the world, though it gives me no pleasure to say so.

Of all the people in the world, I tell the Vet, but before I can say, Of all the people in the world, I probably most resemble you, he said to me:

What is this claptrap? Or: Why did you do it? Or: Now we're cooking with gasoline. Or: Run, don't walk.

That morning after talking to Epstein with the light of his happy family shining in through the phone call, I call the Vet who, like me, lives alone in his one-bedroom dump, emanating only darkness.

Room service, I would say when he picked up the phone.

I'm here. Next time don't call till nine, he says emanating darkness over the phone line.

By the way, I would then say to the Vet before he had a moment to compose himself. I would speak openly with the Vet in the morning on one of my wake-up calls or I would speak openly to him when he was very drunk. The rest of the time I would be guarded with the Vet. Even when I was guarded with the Vet I was still more open with him than I was virtually to anyone else in the world—with the possible exceptions of Epstein, Addison, and now Lucy. Morning was the best time to get information out of the Vet. He was still unformed, untouched—still soft and unguarded from sleep. He had yet to adopt his reflexively hard, formed view of the world. He was still, in many ways, a child, fresh from sleep. In the morning you could get the purest opinion from the Vet. If you wanted to know what the Vet was really thinking you always asked the Vet in the morning.

I met a girl.

Why'd you do that? the Vet asks.

Because I was tired of being in my apartment alone in the heat.

That's it. Now we're cooking with gasoline.

If you didn't get your questions into the Vet first thing in the morning then you waited for the opposite end of the day to come around, in the early morning hours when he was really drunk listening to his *Madama Butterfly* and his bulbous nose was all lit up—for his bulbous nose never told a lie. His nose never told a lie when it was all lit up with emotion.

I met a girl, I say as he puts his *Madama Butterfly* into the cassette player.

One more for the road? he asks.

Sure, why not? It's only one flight of stairs down towards home. I think I can manage.

He opens a beer and lights a cigarette. Where'd I put that tape? Damn. Always misplacing the Goddamn tape. I've got to buy duplicates is what I got to do. By the way, if they ever close Sal's remind me to get that picture of the beautiful boy in his knickers and the bicycle.

Speaking of which, I say, apropos of nothing.

Ah here it is. My beautiful music. Let me put this in. Hold on a second. Ah the beauty, he says with relief. OK, what were you saying?

I met a girl.

Run, don't hide, he says if he's drunk at night and I tell him about Lucy.

Why—you thinking of taking potshots at me?

Never know in this crazy world, let me tell you. Only takes a piece of lead travelling at a few hundred miles an hour to strike you down. Do you realize that? Have you ever even seen a corpse and the damage weapons can inflict on the flesh?

I've heard.

Yes, but until you see you cannot possibly understand.

I don't want to understand.

It's the real world, let me tell you, he'd say. Or he'd say, You talk about reality. You know what reality is for me?

Madama Butterfly?

The smell of corpses. It's a smell you never get out of your nose.

If you can't handle the risk don't come back.

The risk is no problem, I say, my modus operandi urging me forward. I have nothing to lose, and so with nothing to lose we swim to the restful beach of her bed.

Let me tell you about my Lotus Flowers, he says. When I had no reason to go on, they gave me a reason to go on. I needed a reason to go on and they gave me a reason to go on. My Lotus Flowers are the reason why I'm here talking to you today. They gave me a reason to go on living even though I got this stench of corpses in my nose. Do you understand? he would say.

Now you're talking about your corpses, I would point out. I thought we had a moratorium on talking about corpses.

Do you want to know what reality is for me?

Madama Butterfly?

You're always talking about reality, but you for one seem to have a rather poor grasp of reality, if you don't mind me saying.

That's a ridiculous thing to say, I point out to him, trying to be brutally honest.

You don't know the meaning of the word 'ridiculous' until you've gotten this smell of corpses in your nose and are unable to get it out your whole life—unable to escape the smell of corpses even when you sleep. You don't have any idea how ridiculous all of *this*—and he says it like this, *this* making a tremendous hissing sound with his voice—how ridiculous all of *thisss* seems, how ridiculous reality seems with *thisss* smell of corpses—*thisss* permanent stench that never leaves your nose.

Of all the people in the world, I want to tell him, especially when he's emitting nothing but annihilating darkness, I'm most like you. I want to say he and I are exactly alike, but before I can say it—before I can say, It gives me no pleasure to say this, but of everyone I've ever met, I've never met anyone whom I so resemble as you—he says: This music is claptrap. Or: The beauty. Or: Remember to get me that beautiful picture of the boy in his knickers. Don't let Sal's close down without collecting that picture for me.

THIS IS IT, SHE SAYS, opening the door to her place. Take me as I come. I hear my modus operandi in my ear—my inner ear—I won't back down.

What is this claptrap? he asks. Stupid we should waste our time on this. How about we go up to my place to finish a little nightcap? I've my gimpy leg.

Why the hell not? That's what I remember saying: Why the hell not? So I take her as she comes. Garish laughter ensues. I grin and bear it. Nothing else to report here.

That was the last time I saw land, alone in the open water and now I swim through the night alone towards the distant beach—seaweed and carp entangling themselves in my legs. It is night tilting towards deep night when I reach the restful beach, too tired from swimming in the open water alone, the stars overhead lighting my passageway. I wash ashore in the surf entangled in seaweed, carp sucking air through their mouths at the surface of the water. I wash ashore waterlogged as a piece of driftwood too long alone at sea.

There I rest in tattered clothes upon the restful beach and while I rest at the bottom of my wishing well on the beach in tattered clothes he walks in the door and sees us.

Is that him? I ask, smoking the last bit from our cigarette.

One more?

Sure, and so begins our ritual.

Run, she says when he steps through the door. It's him.

But it doesn't look like him.

It's him.

But he's not supposed to come now.

Well he's here anyway. Run, don't walk, and hide.

That's what the Vet always says to me. And I always say back to him: Is someone going to start taking potshots at me?

Of course someone is, she says. And he's that someone, the guy who just walked through the door, Matthew Gliss. He's that someone who's going to start taking potshots at you. Run, don't walk, and hide.

Who is this guy? I ask myself when he steps through the door. Is that him? It must be him. He looked vaguely familiar, though for some reason he looked nothing like the guy in all those photos—the guy who, staring down at me with those beautiful teeth, always made me feel terrible for taking his girl away from him. He looks even less like the guy I vaguely remember—that guy or memory who, upon seeing this person walk through the door, is becoming even more vague. It was never meant to happen like this, I keep telling myself. I only helped her with her credit card, is all. It was hot as hell, is all, and she invited me over to her place, is all. I wasn't going to ruin anyone's relationship. People dying all summer long, dropping dead of the heat. It was a bad omen. All those people alone in their apartments, alone in the heat. Hell, the bank vault was open and the money was on the table. She asked me to come over for a drink so I went over. Not wanting to be alone in the heat, I went over to her apartment for a drink. What would you do? What the hell would you do, positions reversed, if you were in my situation? What, I asked Matthew Gliss, the hell would you do? We're standing together at a bar. I vaguely remember standing there with him.

HEY, HE SAYS, stepping through the door. He's tall, polite, pleasant, a firm handshake, beautiful teeth. He comes over, slaps me on the back. He's vaguely familiar so I buy him a beer.

Can I buy you a drink? I ask.

Sure, I'll take one if you're buying.

Addison, I say to Addison, can you buy this lad and me a beer? That's what I say: Can you buy this lad and me a beer? Then I go with my hands: click click. I do with my fingers, snapping them. It's an old joke I have with Addison that we enjoy very much. Click click and chop chop—just like that he produces a drink for me. It's an old joke, this click click, that Addison enjoys very much. He always laughs when I do my click click I need a drink.

No one else has ever been able to do that and get away with it, Addison tells me the first time I went, jokingly, click click with my fingers. A drink over here.

No one else has ever been able to go click click with me and get away with it. But because I love you like a son, it will be our own personal joke.

Click click. A drink over here, I say, and Addison jumps to get me a beer.

I love you, I tell him time to time. I love you as if you were family, I tell him time to time. Addison's wife is sick with diabetes and in the hospital. He and his wife, Nell, never had a child of their own, and Addison has been fine with that.

I don't feel—I mean Nell and I feel as if we've been happy without children. We've managed just fine. But now that she's in the hospital and off with a leg because of diabetes, I find I miss having children to turn to in this time of crisis.

More than once Addison has told me in absolute confidence: Promise not to tell another soul this. There's not another soul in the bar. All the strangers are off today. It's only Addison and myself. Nascar is on the tube and he pours us a brandy. I'd like to tell you something here, he says. And the way he says it I can tell he wants to tell me something of the utmost seriousness so I don't say a word, only shake my head ever so slightly.

Nell is sick.

I'm sorry, I say.

She caught gangrene on an open wound. Her foot, from diabetes, had an open wound that caught gangrene. Do you know what I'm saying?

I'm sorry, I say. My condolences, I say. I've only met Nell once in my life but I remember a feeling from her. I remember feeling when I met Nell that she was the warmest, most loving human being I'd ever met. I remember thinking to myself when I met Nell that I'd never met someone who was such a gentle soul.

Your wife, I told Addison after having just met Nell, is the most gentle soul in the world. I don't think I've ever met someone so loving.

Yes, Addison says. You made a big impression on her. She took to you immediately.

His comment flattered me beyond belief and I told him so in so many words: Feeling's mutual.

I'm sure. She related to you the way I related to you, he said to me while we were on the topic. And then later when she was in the hospital, her leg lopped off because of gangrene, he told me: You're like a son to me. An heir. Nell feels the same way about you that I do. What I'm saying, he said—and he put his hand on mine, or rather I put my hand on his, and with that he didn't have to complete his sentence, for I knew exactly what he was saying. I was flattered beyond belief by what he left unsaid but what I understood—what we implicitly understood about each other. You're like a son to me, he implied, and I implied to him, by putting my hand on his, that I understood and that he was like a father to me.

You're like an heir to me and my wife, I want you to know, is what he said in so many words. He didn't so much say it as imply it. You're like a son to me and my wife. In this time of trial, with Nell's bad legs, you are of enormous comfort to us. I just want you to know that, he said to me in so many words. Addison, who was eighty-five years of age, was capable of communicating practically anything and everything without saying a word. He was the most communicative noncommunicative person I've ever met.

Cheers, he would say, time to time, and it'd be filled with such meaning, or enjoy, enjoy, filled with such nuance. And what he meant but never so much as said was: Robert, believe you me when I say, you never know how much time you have left—believe you me when you reach my age you know something, a sinister truth. And he used those words, 'sinister truth,' without actually using them, for he implied that the truth, which he'd acquired about life by living eighty-five difficult years, was this:

When it arrives, the end, believe you me, when I say, it arrives all too soon, and this, he would imply without so much as saying it, amounted to one of life's most sinister truths. The truth is, he would imply without so much as saying it, is when you are young like you, you think you have all the time in the world, and in many ways you do have all the time in the world. But when your time is up—even if you live as long as I have been fortunate enough to live—the end arrives too soon. You look around and you say to yourself in shock: How did I get here so soon? I thought I had all the time in the world. I thought my wife, Nell, and I would live forever, and in many ways, we beat the odds. I'm eighty-five, Nell is eighty-two, and we're still kicking. Look, I'm still working, which in this day and age is a miracle. I've been working in one form or another over sixty-three years. And believe me when I say that the end, when it comes, comes too soon. It is one of life's sinister little truths, and you won't understand the meaning of this truth until you yourself are at the end of your rope. It doesn't take all that much time to reach the end of your rope, he would say without saying it but implying it with remarkable circumspection.

Cheers, he would say, but in so saying he'd imply that it doesn't take all that much time to reach the end of your rope. So my advice to you, he would say without saying it, but telling me with his eyes, my advice to you, for I love you like the son I never had, is enjoy. You're progressing beautifully in your life. Enjoy it while you have it, for it's gone before you know it.

NAME'S ROBERT, I tell him, handing him his beer.

Cheers, he says, still looking vaguely familiar. My name is Matthew Gliss.

Cheers back, I say back.

Don't I know you? he says to me. You look vaguely familiar.

Perhaps, I say. It's possible, I tell him. I thought I recognized you as well.

He pats me on the back. Well, good fellow, here's mud in your eye.

Cheers again, I say.

And he says: It was a party, wasn't it? Didn't I see you at a party or something?

Could be, I say. Anything's possible.

I'm sure it's that, he says, patting me on the back. Déjà vu. Here, let me get you one, he says, throwing his beer back. Thirsty as hell tonight. The heat. And he, like I, goes click click with his fingers. Another round here, barkeep.

Addison's a sport. He's a beautiful man. Always so cheerful —such a cheerful fellow with his mantra, cheers, saying it all day long and the days bleeding into years.

He pours two brandies. These are on me, Addison says, such a sport. Here, you'll enjoy this, he says, not minding that someone else went click click—someone other than I.

In all of my years, Addison once told me, no one but you has ever gotten away with that click click thing with the fingers. But that's OK. It'll be our own private little joke.

We sat there on a blazing hot afternoon, the air conditioner rattling in the window but producing precious little cool air. He tells me—the air conditioner rattling for all it's worth on such a blazing hot day—about his wife, Nell, leg lopped off. Gangrene, he says quietly, as if the mere saying of it were enough to contaminate the air we're sitting in. Then, as an afterthought, asks: Ever smell a rotted foot?

Never, I say with elaborate politeness.

Be honest with you—reminds me of my war years working as a medic for the Red Cross. Reminds me of my shovel-and-bag days if you know what I mean.

Just then I grow terrified that Addison, such a cheerful fellow you'd never know he's a World War II veteran, so cheerful—always saying cheers—you'd never know that he's capable, like the Vet, of pulling out a few of his own corpses. But he's like a father to me and the corpses stored up so long alone in his brain unsaid because he's such a cheerful fellow, always saying cheers, all day long pouring drinks, cheers, spreading good cheer as he pours his drinks, such a fatherly figure that I try, in the face of his corpses, to be like Epstein. Be like Epstein, I tell myself, as Addison begins talking about his World War II corpses. Do as Epstein would do and be as solicitous as possible, I tell myself.

If you want to say it, say it, I tell Addison cheerfully, trying my utmost to be absolutely solicitous. If you want to tell me about those war years, way back when, then shoot. Go right on ahead. If it'll make you feel better.

No, Addison says, forget that. But the way he says it, implying so much more than the word itself—'no,' he says and that no a corpse, a rotted corpse stored so long alone in his brain unsaid. No—and all of the corpses rotting on the field, the attending effluvia. I was a shovel-and-bag man, if you know what I mean. Have you ever smelled a corpse? No. A field of corpses and their attending effluvia. A field of corpses all bound up in that sinister little no. And the sad look on his face. The brutally truthful brutally sad look on his forlorn face, his wife's leg lopped off, diabetes, the smell of gangrene in the hot air. The gangrenously brutal truth of his sad face forces me to go click click, and it was the first time I had ever gone click click with him, never before daring such a move, and when I go click click with my fingers, snapping him out of it, he smiles at me as if I were a son of his. You're an heir with that one. Like a son. Nell feels the same way about you that I do, he says to me. You'll inherit everything we have for that one, he says to me. Then off he goes, chop chop, to get us a brandy and he's light as ever on his legs. He's just as spry as can be. Such a cheerful man, pouring us our brandies. Cheers, he says, pouring himself a shot.

Cheers, I say, holding up my glass. Then bottoms up a swipe at the lips and enjoy, enjoy all around and the days melt into years.

CLICK CLICK, BARKEEP, Matthew Gliss says, having upended his beer, while I, emulating him, upend mine.

Addison's a sport when Matthew Gliss goes click click with his fingers. Addison's an eminently beautiful man. He pours three brandies, one for the each of us. These are on me, he says. Here, he says to Matthew Gliss, who has such a beautiful smile. You'll enjoy this.

What—my money's no good in this place? Matthew Gliss says dropping a twenty on the bar. First him buying me a drink, then you. Who are you guys anyway? The charm brigade?

Your money's no good if you're a friend of Robert's. Cheers! Addison says.

Cheers, I say.

Cheers.

Everybody clicking glasses.

Then I turn to Matthew and ask him, apropos of nothing, a theoretical question.

You seem a decent guy to me, I say to him.

Wait till you get to know me, he says.

But I want to ask you.

Shoot.

If you walked into a bank.

If I walked into a bank. Go on.

Say it's a perfect summer afternoon. No—say it's hot as hell and you're dying of the heat. So you walk into a bank to cash a check but the bank vault is open and nobody is looking.

Is this a trick question?

No, it's a theoretical question. Theoretically, I ask him, if you walked into a bank and saw there was nobody else in the bank but you—let's say the safe is open and there are piles of bills sitting in the safe—my question to you is what would you do?

This is what I ask Matthew Gliss while sitting at the bar drinking brandies: If the safe was open and nobody was looking, what would you do? Would you turn around and go home, or would you say: Shit, why the hell not? The bank is open. It's hot as hell. The money is on the table so why the hell not?

This is a trick question, right?

Not a trick question, I say. Just what would you do if you suddenly saw the bank vault open and piles of cash and nobody around to see you take it? What would you do?

I suppose I'd take it, he says. Why not? All things being equal. I mean if I knew there was nobody looking and the cash was just sitting there in the open for the taking, I suppose I'd just take the cash. If it were untraceable, I suppose, realistically speaking, I'd have no problem stepping up to the bank vault, provided no one was monitoring me, and taking the cash, provided the cash was untraceable. Why?

No reason. I just wanted to know.

What would you do?

I'd do like you, I suppose, I say to him. I'd do like you. I'd just take the money and run, and then I'd find a beach somewhere and a place nearby to rest.

Sounds like a plan, he says raising his glass. Cheers.

Cheers, I say.

To banks and beaches.

That's it, I say. Now you're cooking with gasoline. To banks and beaches.

IS THAT HIM? I ask in the confusion of the moment.

We're smoking a cigarette in the dark when he steps through the door.

It's him, she says. Run, don't walk!

It looks nothing like him, I say.

It's him.

It doesn't even look anything like the man I vaguely remember —the man who used to slap me on the back every time I saw him. The man I bought beers for one time or another.

It's him.

And so it was him bursting through the door and between the moment he burst through the door and the moment he stepped into the bedroom to get a closer look at me I had time enough to hear my modus operandi. This modus operandi, I swear, I tell myself lying there next to her on the restful beach, will one day be my downfall. It will be the end of me. I'm sure of it. It's another bad omen that I'll overleap but I really should listen to my instincts. It's not a bad omen for nothing, I tell myself. It's a bad omen because it's trying to tell you something. If it weren't trying to warn you of the potential ills that lie ahead, it wouldn't be a bad omen. But this modus operandi is death to bad omens because when bad omens pop up to warn me, 'I won't back down' causes me to overleap them and therefore my modus operandi, I'm quite sure of it, will one day be the death of me. This 'I won't back down' I overleap as easily as I overleap all of the other bad omens she has placed in front of me—overleaped even though all my instincts tell me not to overleap.

If the risk is too great, you can always back down, she tells me.

No, I say. Then there's that mysterious smile of hers that photos fail to capture. She flashes it and while she flashes it I'm pushed into saying: Of course I won't back down. Not after this afternoon. I promise.

Good, she says, her mysterious smile flashing. Because I had a lovely time here today and I would love for you to come back. Who knows, she adds no doubt to make me happy, where this may lead?

He steps in closer to see what his eyes are telling him but what his brain because it is locked in habit or because it is trained by love to trust her is refusing to believe. His eyes are telling him that another dwarf will soon be tattooed to the back of his fiancée even though he refuses to believe that the dwarfs she tattoos to her back have any correlation to real-life suitors. He refuses to believe that each dwarf on the back of his fiancée represents a suitor whom she's gone to while she's been with him.

How long have you been together?

Forever—can't tell you even if I could. Wouldn't know even if I could. The fan blows hot wind across our elongated or foreshortened or overheated bodies.

Why are you doing this tattoo? Matthew Gliss asks her as the tattoo slowly grows and gathers a life of its own on her back. The tattoo started out simple and small but slowly over the years it has become her life's obsession, gathering a life of its own.

Why are you doing this tattoo? Matthew asks her as he realizes the tattoo is taking on a life of its own on the back of Lucy, his fiancée, becoming an obsession of hers.

Because my life is boring, she'll say to him time to time if she even deigns to answer his question at all. Or she'll say: Matthew, I do it because I'm bored. Or, Because I feel I have nothing better to do.

Why are you doing this tattoo? Matthew Gliss asks.

Because I'm bored. I feel I have nothing better to do.

Who are these dwarfs anyway? he asks knowing deep down who they are—her suitors—even though he refuses to believe his own intuitions.

What's an intuition? he asks himself or perhaps he asks a coworker of his down at the office where he plies his trade as a banker. Hey, John, he says to his office mate. Got a second?

Sure.

A question for you not related to the PepsiCo. account. In your opinion what's an intuition?

I don't know, John says. An omen, I suppose. An omen of some sort. That's what I'd say. An intuition is an omen.

And what about trusting them? Should one trust one's intuitions?

Sure, why not? John says. Trust your intuitions. Then he makes a sign with his hand. Trust the Force, Luke.

Or Matthew Gliss tells himself time to time in pertinence to her tattoo: Who are these dwarfs? Why is this tattoo taking on a life of its own?

He'll ask her the same question: Come on, tell me about this damn tattoo. Who are these dwarfs? Just cartoon figures? Is that it?

She knows he knows but will play dumb if he plays dumb and so says, Yeah, cartoon characters. Why not? Do you like them?

Not particularly. Then he asks, Do these dwarfs on your back represent anyone from your life? Is this tattoo symbolic of anything?

No, she says. *Ceci n'est pas un symbole,* she says. It's just an image I've been going with. The whole tattoo is something that's just been evolving. It's a piece of artwork really, she tells him. A cartoon. Nothing to be taken too seriously. I do it because I'm bored. I feel I have nothing better to do.

Or other times, Matthew Gliss asks her in pertinence to her tattoo, which is slowly taking on a life of its own: Why are you spending all of this time and money defacing yourself with this damned tattoo?

Because my life is boring, she says to him. I want to do something to distinguish it.

To distinguish what?

My life.

You think this tattoo distinguishes your life? he asks her. He's still got that beautiful smile with those beautiful teeth. But while he's talking to her it's even more beautiful than it is in the photographs. How does this tattoo distinguish your life? I don't understand.

I feel I've always been a blank canvas, she says to Matthew Gliss with the beautiful smile. I feel I've always been a blank canvas waiting for a piece of artwork, and now—with this tattoo artist that I've found who is doing an inspired job and this image that is developing on my back—I feel I've found what I've been looking for: this tattoo. It's something that has evolved gradually, but as it's evolved I find I've become attached to it. I think it distinguishes me.

Forget about your tattoo, he tells her one night when she leaves the apartment for a visit with the tattoo artist. You're wasting your time and money.

Forget about me, she tells him one night when she leaves her apartment for a visit with the tattoo artist and he says to her in his cutting way, Forget about your tattoo. You're wasting your time and money.

Forget about me, she says.

You think you can tell me to forget about you, he says in his cutting way, and expect me to do it?

As a matter of fact, yes.

You expect to get away with this?

Sure, why not?

How long have you been together?

I can't tell you how many years we've been together. It seems like forever.

Have there been others?

Funny you should ask, she says. There have been seven others, she tells me. She refers to her Technicolor tattoo that scared the hell out of me when I first saw it, only moments earlier the scent of gasoline still fresh on my fingers. There have been seven others since Matthew Gliss, she said matter-of-factly. As you can see, they're all represented right there on my back.

And what does he say about this tattoo?

What can he say? He has to take me as I come or leave me.

WE'RE LYING IN THE HEAT of her apartment, the fan blowing hot air across our foreshortened or elongated torsos. It's boiling hot. We're both in our underwear smoking cigarettes.

One more?

Sure, why not? The ember from the cigarette glows in the night.

I don't know how long I've been with him, she says, picking up the thread of a conversation that she's constantly unspooling then respooling. I hate talking about this kind of stuff with her. Like talking to the Vet about his corpses. But I sit and listen. One night he says to me: Forget about your damn tattoo. I say back: Forget about me. That's how I got this, she says, pointing to her chipped tooth.

You think you can get away with talking like this to me?

Yes—drags me into the bathroom, smashes my face against the bathtub, chipping my tooth, the violence of it just shocking.

I hate talking about this stuff with her so I try to switch the subject. I want to confess something to her that's huge. So I begin by telling her: May I be honest with you?

Do you want me to shoot you?

No.

Then be honest.

I feel that my life—I feel my life . . .

But she switches the subject. It's my life here, Robert—she tells me while I'm swimming in the bottom of my wishing well, swimming for so long, only the stars illuminate my passageway to the restful beach—which was almost snuffed out, because I told him to forget about me.

Well, I say, forget about him.

Not so easy, she says. To just say 'bye' to someone like that.

We're lying in her bed smoking one last cigarette, the ember from the cigarette illuminating the night before us. She smiles her chipped-tooth mysterious smile and talks: Drags me into the bathroom and smashes my face against the bathtub, chipping my tooth.

It's part of your mystery, I tell her. Your chipped tooth lends a bit of mystery to your smile.

It's ugly, she says, and one day I want to cap it. One day when I have the money.

And I've asked her in the past because you see her pictures showed one thing, a beautiful smile, but her smile shows a different thing, a chipped tooth. So I'd ask her time to time out of curiosity.

So out of curiosity, I'd ask her, how'd you chip your tooth?

In idle moments, a silence drifting between us, lying in the heat in our underwear, I'd ask, apropos of nothing, fan blowing hot air across our elongated or foreshortened torsos: Tell me, how'd you chip that tooth?

I don't remember, she'll say. Or she'll say: I slipped on a slick piece of ice and cracked it. It happened this past winter, and I've been broke lately and unable to fix it.

Don't you have dental coverage?

Where I work—are you kidding? Do you think the Greek would offer dental care? He barely pays my salary.

But one day, apropos of nothing, I asked her how she chipped that tooth, and apropos of nothing, she told me Matthew Gliss did it. I tried to change the subject once she got onto Matthew Gliss, but it was like talking to the Vet about his corpses.

Have you ever smelled one?

Have you?

Yes, and believe you me, it's a smell you never forget.

How'd you chip your tooth?

Matthew Gliss did it. He chipped it. You asked. Now I've answered. Happy?

I'm sorry, I said—not knowing what else to say, feeling cornered.

I suppose you want to know how it happened too?

Not necessary, I said.

Since you don't want to know about the horrors of war, let me tell you about the whores of war.

Since you continue to ask, I'll tell. If that's what you want. I'll be perfectly honest and tell.

Why do you bother with that tattoo?

Because I'm bored. I feel I have nothing to do.

Why do you bother with that tattoo?

Because my life is uselessly aimless.

The safe was open, the money on the table, is all. It was hot as hell is all. I was curious, is all.

Want to come to my place?

Hot as hell. Why not? I say. Why the hell not?

I follow her in my AMC Hornet to her place. It's hot as hell with all the windows open in my car. We pull up to her place, so derelict it makes me concerned that this whole thing is going to be a mistake.

Don't do it, I tell myself. You're stepping into a hornet's nest, I tell myself as I pull in behind her at her apartment. An abandoned swimming pool is growing weeds and a tree rises from a crack in the concrete. The apartment complex is in disrepair. Go home, I tell myself, while you still have a chance. She gets out of her car, closes the door behind her. Nonsense, I tell myself. Go home alone in this heat? It's being alone in this heat that makes both being alone and the heat equally untenable.

Being alone is one thing, I tell the Vet. We're in the car on the way to the track. And being in the heat is one thing. But being alone and in the heat—I can't take it anymore.

I agree, the Vet says, soberly.

If I were only alone . . .

Yes.

I could take it.

So could I.

If it were only the heat and I weren't alone, I could take it.

I agree.

But to be alone in the heat alone is too much.

Ha! Ha! That's it. Now we're cooking with gasoline.

Why'd you do it?

Do what?

You know what.

Alone in the heat alone.

That's it. Bravo. Now we're cooking with gasoline.

Up the stairs to her apartment. Should I turn back, go home to my apartment alone in the heat alone? Yes, but then I hear it—my modus operandi—and it tells me, in a way no other song ever has, how to move through this moment. Go home or continue forward? Continue forward, it says. Don't back down. I look over my shoulder one last time at the derelict pool. Why the hell not? I tell myself, swimming alone at the bottom of my wishing well, water water everywhere and not a beer to drink.

Later when I'm at Sal's, when I pull myself out of the wishing well, swimming so long alone by myself alone, I tell Addison that I met her at the gas station while gassing up my car.

He doesn't ask, Why'd you do it? but merely smiles and pats me on the back, pours us each a brandy. Cheers, he says. Here, he says, pouring each of us a brandy. Cheers. You got yourself some, he says. Congratulations. Enjoy it while it lasts, he says, tipping his glass back. Because these sorts of things—

Yes—

Can be gone before you know it.

IS THIS WHY YOU GOT INTO THIS? I ask myself, lying in bed next to her talking about Matthew Gliss. Because it can be gone before I know it, my blood ax collecting dust and rust in the corner while the light changes from dawn to dusk and all the seasons passing by while I, against my will, get caught up in these vicious tube-watching cycles that take no prisoners—or swimming in my well, water water everywhere and not a drop to drink. Is this why I did it? I ask myself, lying in bed next to her talking about Matthew Gliss. Because I have a blood ax that's collecting dust and rust in the corner.

My Mystic, Epstein—I love him for his purity. Of everyone I know, no one is as pure and beautiful as Epstein. I take Epstein's lessons to heart. I don't know why I take Epstein's lessons to heart, but his lessons are beautiful lessons so I take them to heart.

When we went fishing, for instance, and we most loved to fish for carp, and if he or I caught a carp he was so solicitous to the fish. He only used chrome-plated nonbarbed steel hooks, and they had to be razor sharp. Epstein insisted on razor-sharp hooks because he thought any hook less than razor sharp would inflict undue pain onto the fish.

Be careful, he would say as I was hauling a fish out of the water with the net, not to inflict undue pain unto the fish. He sometimes talked biblically. I wish thee not to inflict undue pain unto the fish. Take care not to killeth the carp and if it should be kilt, do so without inflicting undue pain. If you must needs killeth the carp, do so quickly by severing the head.

He was careful not to inflict undue pain unto the carp and the razor-sharp hook without a barb was, in his opinion, the most humane way to catch fish, and the carp seemed to appreciate Epstein's solicitousness. Whenever we caught a fish, we'd gently net it and pull it out of the water and, just as gently, I'd spit in the fish's eye for luck, and after the benediction, 'Carpe diem,' I'd let the fish very gently back into the river: a twitch of the tail, a swirl of water, and it was gone, re-merged with the murky depths. And I would turn and say to Epstein: Can you believe they call these rough fish?

And Epstein would say: There's nothing rough about them.

It was all very mystical and beautiful and I wished that I could bring all of Epstein's mystical approach to the world into my own life, but I didn't understand his mystical approach nor did his wife, Meg, who had known Epstein ever since they were childhood sweethearts.

He's very mystical, I would say.

Our Mystic, she would point out. I really don't understand it, but I stand in awe.

We all stand in awe, I would say. He's awesome.

We're down by the water fishing for carp and just before he becomes a stone I tell him again: May I be honest with you?

Shoot.

I feel my life is useless. And while he becomes a stone I tell him about my blood ax collecting dust and rust in the corner.

It just sits there in the corner of my apartment collecting dust and rust, I tell him. My life is useless and aimless. I feel I'm without direction.

Life is useless, he says to me, becoming a stone. It is useless like a stone or like a gift, he says to me, becoming a stone, which is like a gift to me, watching him become a stone, one with all the animate and inanimate creatures in a sacred unity. Get used to it, he says. Life is useless. Nothing at all to do about it.

Easy for him to say, I'll say to myself. Other times he'll say: It's easy to die alone once we have lived our life course. And I would say to myself upon hearing this: Easy for you to say—you who have a wife and children—but what about me? My blood ax collecting dust and rust in the corner, water water everywhere and not a beer to drink.

Easy to say, I tell him while he becomes inanimate as a stone. But difficult to do.

Maybe so, he replies as he becomes one with the animate and inanimate in a sacred unity with all things. But the rewards for doing so are incalculable.

WHY ARE YOU DOING THIS? I distinctly remember asking myself, stepping over the berm that naturally separates us, hot as hell, climbing the stairs to her apartment, my modus operandi urging me forward despite the bad omen of her derelict swimming pool. We're lying there in the heat, where the air is incredibly still and hot, though not fetid. Later it would become fetid and when it became fetid I would say to myself: Notice this room, how fetid it's becoming. Its fetidness is a bad omen. You should turn, go back down the stairs. But my modus operandi urges me forward. She touches the fan on with her toe then strokes the back of my calf and begins telling me her life story, which she repeats over and over again. I lie there patiently listening, though it gives me just as much pain to hear her tell of Matthew as it gives me pain to listen to the Vet tell of his corpses, *Die Meistersinger* playing on his cassette player.

I've noticed with you, I tell the Vet time to time over a nightcap, that this beautiful music of yours—what is it you call it?—*Die Meistersinger*?

Wagner, yes.

I've noticed Wagner almost always leads you to your corpses. I've noticed too that *Madama Butterfly*—

Puccini, yes.

That Puccini almost always leads you finally to a discussion of the whores of war. Why is that?

I dispute your observation, he says, late at night or early in the morning, still hardened by the day. And so I know there's no getting an answer out of him until he is vulnerable from sleep in the morning or late, late at night when he's had too much to drink.

I've noticed, I tell the Vet time to time, one tape makes you discuss the horrors of war. The other tape makes you discuss the whores of war.

There's more to my conversation than these two items.

No there isn't, I say, being brutally honest. What's worse, without your tapes, you become conversationally useless.

Not true.

Yes, true.

No.

Yes.

No.

Do you know anything about Glocks? I ask, changing the subject, hoping against hope to avoid another conversation about corpses.

I'll collect one if that's what you're saying.

All I'm asking is what do you know about them?

Say no more. I'll collect one for you in a few weeks.

That's not what I'm saying.

Then what?

When I didn't answer, he reiterated: A few weeks. Give me a few weeks, that's all. You say you want a 10mm. I thought they only made 9s. But if you want a 10, a 10 it'll be. That should be a very interesting weapon to collect.

Then later—on the way to the track after having pulled me out of a vicious tube-watching cycle—he says to me: You know that Glock you asked about?

We're on our way to the track when he asks me: Remember that Glock you asked about? The 10mm?

Yes.

Well, I've gone and collected one for you.

He says to me, apropos of nothing, one day on the way to the track: Good news, Robert.

Tell me.

You know that Glock you asked about?

Yes.

Well, I've collected one for you. And it's a 10mm. Nearly impossible to get my hands on a 10 but I collected one nevertheless.

How'd you do it? I ask him, staring out the window, feeling my heart drop. How'd you collect it? For I still found it hard to believe that the Vet had such networks into the world that he could go ahead and collect a Glock.

Oh I have my ways, he says. What do you say, he says, we go to the dump after the fifth and go plink around with it a bit? How'd you like to waste a little time popping off a few rounds? He laughs. Shoot some things with it.

What do you say? If you're game, he says, I'm game.

We'll play it by ear, I say.

And then after the fifth when we've both run out of money—me on accident, the Vet on purpose because he wants to get the hell off the track for the day and head over to the dump while there is still light—he says, Let's get the hell out of here, while there's still light. I know a good place to shoot this thing off. What do you say?

What do you say? I say, and so off we go to the dump and as I drive in the car next to the Vet on the way to the dump, I tell myself: I wouldn't even own a Glock even if I could. Of everything I could think of doing with my time in this world, shooting off a Glock seems the least desirable thing in the world.

A beautiful piece of mechanicals, he says, pulling it out of the glove compartment to show me.

It's a small gun, smaller than I imagined it would be and he's got a case of rounds, which are heavier than I thought they would be. Ever use one of these things before? he asks me, and when I don't immediately answer him, holding the gun in my hand as if mesmerized by it, he says as an afterthought: No I don't suppose you would have ever had an opportunity to use one of these things. Don't worry, he says. I'll show you everything you need to know. Once you get your hand on this thing and use it you'll see just as surely as day is day that what you have here is a beautiful little piece of mechanicals.

Later, when he's popping it off, squeezing off several rounds at a time, I hear him mutter under his breath: The beauty.

Plink. Plink. Plink. The Goddamned beauty. Plink. What a beautiful piece of mechanicals. Plink. Plink. Jesus Christ this thing is a beautiful piece—an amazing piece of mechanicals. Plink. God, Robert, you are going to love this thing here. Plink. Plink. Plink. Plink. Got it! Jesus, you are just going to love this thing! I do believe you are absolutely going to love this Glock here! Plink. Plink. Plink. Plink. Plink.

IS THIS WHY YOU DID THIS? I ask myself, fan blowing hot air across our elongated or foreshortened overheated bodies. Are you doing this to become privy to the lives of this strange woman with a mysterious chip-toothed smile and Matthew Gliss? Why, I ask myself, did I go and do this—climb the stairs to her apartment and wash up on the shores of her bed on one of the hottest days of the century? When no answer is forthcoming I tell myself: I did it because there was money on the table and it was hot as hell. It was not about taking this woman away from Matthew Gliss, whom I vaguely recall was a good guy, always slapping me on the back.

Why don't you stay home tonight? Give up on your tattoo—it's ghoulish.

Why don't you give up on me, she tells me she told him.

Why do you think you can say that and get away with it?

Because I think I can tell you what I want.

That's where you're mistaken.

I'm leaving.

Come here.

Drags me back into the apartment screaming and shouting 'bullshit!' Who knows what the neighbors think. The violence he shows to me is explosive. The violence is so explosive, I don't know how to respond to it. It's so explosive, it shocks me into submission.

I'm leaving, she tells me she told him.

Bullshit—come here!

Like the Vet telling about his corpses, she tells again and again about her chipped tooth. Drags me into the bathroom screaming and shouting 'bullshit!' And when I feel cornered by her mysterious smile I remain cornered and reflect her smile back at her best as I can.

Tells me, screaming and shouting, holding my head above the bathtub: You think your lousy tattoo is worth this? Drags me by the hair into the bathroom. The violence he shows is a violence I have never seen before. You think your tattoo is worth this, he says, dragging me into the bathroom by the hair. And who are these dwarfs anyway? he asks. Drags me by the hair into the bathroom. The violence he shows is sudden and frightening. I don't know how to respond to it. My instinct is to become passive and mute. You think this tattoo is worth this? he asks again. Answer me, he says again. You think this tattoo is worth it? The violence is so sudden, it surprises me. It's so sudden and so violent, which surprises me. But also I'm surprised at my response: passive and mute. Drags me by the hair while I'm passive. Answer me! Don't just lie there on the floor. Answer me.

Mute.

How long have you been with him?

Too long.

Answer me. Violence is so great, so sudden that I become passive and mute. I don't know why I become passive and mute. Perhaps a better strategy would be to pry myself loose and leave—take my own advice: run, don't walk—but the violence is something I've never encountered before. I wasn't brought up to deal with violence, she says to me, telling me about how she chipped her tooth.

She's looking in the mirror one morning combing her hair. I'm lying in her bed, watching her reflection in the mirror, one hand dangling in the pool of my wishing well. She talks to the mirror, talking to me.

Are you talking to me or talking to the mirror? I ask.

Turns on her radio to a dance station. Talking to my radio, she says.

Where are you from anyway? I ask. The enchanted forest? She's naked in front of the mirror, combing her hair, the shocking Technicolor tattoo of the woman and the seven dwarfs who are not Snow White and *the* Seven Dwarfs but her—Lucy—and her seven. The tattoo is alive on her flesh, which is also alive.

I was brought up to live and let live, that's all, she says to me. Those were the values I was raised with, she tells me, talking to the mirror while talking to me or to the radio as the case may be. My father was one of those fathers—never raised his voice. Always told me: Live and let live. He also said: Do unto others first. The golden rule was a very important rule in our house. You want to be successful, he would tell us, follow the golden rule. He also liked to say: Be the first to give and forgive. Always be the first to give and to forgive. Those who give and forgive receive the truest rewards, he would say. That was my father's philosophy. Growing up, every new day presented new opportunities for my father to tell us his philosophy. You want to know what my philosophy is on this? he would say when there was only one piece of candy and two of us wanted it. He would whisper into my ear: Let go of your piece of candy—give and you shall receive the truest gift of all. I loved my father. Or when someone did something awful to me—like once a girl on my block who was older than me hit me on the head with a bottle. It shattered and cut my scalp and I never did know why she hit me over the head with that bottle. When I went home, bleeding down my face, my father asked what happened and when I told him, he said: I want you to go over to her house right now and tell that girl you forgive her. But, Dad, I pointed out, she hasn't even apologized to me. It doesn't matter, he would say. You must be proactive and be the first to forgive. He was the most giving and forgiving man I ever knew. He told us to believe in love. Learn to love, he would say, and you will live a happy, prosperous life. Other times he would quote statistics to us: Do you know, he would say to us, research says that those who smile, love, and give live on average twenty years longer than those who frown, hate, and take! What side of the equation do you want to be on? he would ask us. My father believed from the very beginning that the world was flawed. The world is flawed, he would tell us. It's our job to make it right. That's why you must smile, love, and give. Do unto others first. Always be the first to give. I tried to live by what he told us but I failed somewhere along the way. Impossible to live up to my father. Got caught up with the wrong people I suppose, she says to me. Shouldn't have stayed all this time with Matthew Gliss. Should have left him the moment I set eyes on him, but I stayed. One doesn't very easily say 'bye' to a person like Matthew Gliss. It's only a tattoo, I wanted to tell Matthew, but his violence came so sudden I didn't know how to speak. Can you imagine, me of all people, made mute by the terror that his sudden violence caused in me?

Do you think this tattoo is worth it? Answer me! Grabs me by the hair, lifts my head so I can look at him. Look at me and answer me! When I don't answer he throws my head away, smashing it against the edge of the tub. Blood everywhere. Teeth embedded into my lip. A shocking pain. He gets up and urinates on me. He actually urinates on me. There, he says. Maybe this will keep you from going to see your tattoo artist. Maybe this will teach you a lesson.

He returned two days later, penitent. Take me back, he pleaded. *Always be the first to give and the first to forgive.* Those were my father's words so I forgave him and gave him another chance. I'll have this tooth fixed too, soon as I get a chance. So if he ever steps in here and sees the two of us together, do us both a favor, Robert, run the hell out of here as fast as you can run. Don't believe for a moment that you can talk your way out of a confrontation with him.

But come on, I say. I swear I've met him before one time or another and he always seemed perfectly reasonable to me.

How well did you know him? she asks.

Only vaguely.

Well if you really knew him, if you knew him like I know him, and not just vaguely, you would see that he's not someone to mess around with. He wouldn't take you being here with me very lightly at all. He'd kill you is what I'm saying. You'd be killed if he caught you here in this room with me.

AND SO I'M PLUNGED BACK into the abyss where I started wondering how it's possible for someone—how, even for someone like Matthew Gliss, who seems decent enough, all things considered—to take my life away for something so innocent as casual sex during a blazing hot summer. I didn't even mean for it to go this far, I tell myself. Only followed her home to her place for a cold drink.

What are you doing right now?

No plans to speak of, I say.

Want to come over to my place and cool off with a drink?

I had nothing to do for the day or for the rest of my life for that matter so what the hell, and I think that's exactly what I told her: What the hell.

I climb the stairs to her apartment, the derelict swimming pool behind me as if I'm climbing out of my own wishing well, for I've been swimming so long water water everywhere and not a drop to drink and as I climb the stairs to her apartment I feel it like a bad omen. I feel it but can't quite put into words exactly what I feel. Later, I would come to see that what I felt climbing those stairs that day—the bad omen that I felt but was unable to put into words—was Matthew Gliss. I sensed even as I was walking up the stairs to her place that there would be somebody, only I didn't know who, and for reasons that I couldn't explain I sensed a weapon would be involved. Later I would see it would be Matthew Gliss sitting at her kitchen table eating a slice of bread and drinking a glass of orange juice. But at the time it was just a bad omen that I couldn't put into words. This is a bad omen, I tell myself walking up the stairs to her apartment, the derelict swimming pool behind us, because one day—and I can see it all so very clearly walking up the steps behind her—because one day you will walk up these stairs and there will be someone and from that moment on, I say to myself, nothing will ever be the same in my life. Your life, I say to myself, walking up the stairs behind her to her apartment, is one thing now, but it will be something else completely different, walking up these stairs, seeing someone here at her apartment. Your life is this, I tell myself, walking up the stairs to her apartment, my modus operandi urging me forward, but once you cross the threshold your life will be something else entirely, and I saw it then as if it were a premonition. Saw it as if it were now and not later, climbing the stairs, a weapon of some sort in hand. Why a weapon? I ask myself, climbing the stairs to her apartment. And then later when she says, He has a Glock—believe me the damage that thing can do—I begin to see that the weapon will be something I wouldn't own even if I could. There will be a weapon, I say to myself, climbing the stairs to her apartment. Only I don't know what type of weapon. Later, lying in her bed, the fan blowing hot air across our elongated or foreshortened bodies, she tells me: He has a 10mm Glock is what he calls it.

And then later still, a stranger working the bar, the Vet and I sitting near the fireplace, I ask him, apropos of nothing in particular: Out of curiosity, do you know anything about Glocks?

And he being who he is, saying, Why? You want me to collect one for you?

Wouldn't even own a Glock even if I could, I tell myself, and he asks me again: Would be simple to collect one for you if that's what you want. I'd love to do it for you.

When no answer is forthcoming, he says: Consider it done. I'll collect a 10mm. I thought they only made 9s, but if it's a 10 you want I'll collect a 10. No problem.

And then later, after the fifth race at the track, our tickets torn and dropped to our feet: What do you say? he says to me. Want to get out of here and go plinking at the dump while there's still light?

Hey, Robert, he says, tearing up his race tickets. Let's get the hell out of here while there's still light. I want to show you how this thing works.

Here it is, he says, driving on the way to the dump, pulling it out of the glove compartment. It's smaller and more compact than I believe things like this could be, and the box of rounds, which I also pull out, is heavier than I imagined it might be.

Only takes a piece of lead travelling a few hundred miles an hour, really, he says, lighting one cigarette off another. Ah forget about it, he says. Forget the hell about it, he says, lighting one cigarette off another. Don't take my word for it. You'll see what I'm saying. Plink around a little with it at the dump. You'll see it doesn't take much to undo a life.

I see it already going up the stairs to her apartment, long before there's anything to see, that there will be a weapon involved. And why do you say this? I say to myself, going up the stairs to her apartment. I say it because I sense it and I sense it because of the derelictness of her apartment complex. It's the abandoned pool and the rusted stairs that make me believe a weapon will be involved, I tell myself, walking up the stairs behind her to her place. And then I say to myself: But what about your place? Your place is no better than hers, I tell myself, going up the stairs to her place. No different whatsoever, and if positions were reversed—if it was she coming to your place instead of you going to hers—would you still think a weapon will one day be involved? Impossible to say, I say to myself. No telling, I say to myself, walking up the stairs to her apartment, feeling like I've suddenly stepped into a hornet's nest.

And what would she think, going up the stairs to your place? I ask myself, going up the stairs to her place. Would she also think that this is bound to end in blood? And how wrong would she be, going up the back steps to my one-bedroom dump, to assume that only something malevolent would result from entering into a dump like mine? What could possibly happen, her coming up the backstairs to my apartment, other than two souls washed up on a beach swimming so long alone in the heat alone? So why not go up the rusted stairs to her derelict place, I tell myself, and forget that anything malevolent will result from this? Why not realize that going up the rusted stairs to her place is only going up the backstairs to her place and nothing more? Why not realize that it's hot as hell, is all? Tired of swimming alone in the heat alone, is all. Why not just realize that and let the rest go? That's what I say to myself, just after I hear my modus operandi kick in.

Any plans? she asks after I gas up her car.

None to speak of.

What do you say you come over to my place for a drink?

What the hell. Why not? And so off we go, she in her RX-7 and I in my AMC Hornet, up the stairs to her apartment, where I sense it like a premonition that one day in the not-too-distant future there will be a weapon involved. Whatever comes of this, I say to myself, going up the stairs to her apartment, this much can be said: It's going to end in no good.

That's when I hear my song coming from a car in the parking lot or an apartment window. Too late to back down now, I say to myself, after I've heard my modus operandi. What's more, I've gone this far, I tell myself. And even if I want to turn back, I reason, how in hell would I explain it to her? Would I say: Oh gee, you know what? I forgot I had to do something. Do you mind if we get together another day?

Do I say, Hey, let's get together another day. Now's not a good time?

Sorry, can't do this, I say, going up the rusted stairs to her apartment.

What do you mean? she asks, looking at me incredulously.

I've got plans. I forgot but my friend Epstein and I—it's this ritual we have sitting on the muddy banks of the Des Plaines River fishing for carp, me nattering away about the uselessness of my life while he slowly becomes a stone in the virginal wilderness.

That's not acceptable, she says. Impossible, she says, flashing me that mysterious smile, which suddenly makes me proud as hell, and you know she's right. How could she possibly be wrong, flashing me that mysterious smile of hers? How in hell could she possibly ever be wrong? I can't back down, so I follow her up to her place despite the bad omens. Forget about the bad omens, I tell myself even as I overleap them. You only live once, I hear Addison tell me time and time again. Take what you can get and enjoy, I hear Addison tell me time and time again. So what the hell, I say to myself, and up I go to her place, overleaping yet another bad omen.

Why'd you do it? the Vet asks when I come back to my place. He's standing outside my door, waiting for me in the heat of the hallway. He can't believe I've been gone so long. He's worried that I've become a corpse alone somewhere in the heat.

Why'd you do it? he asks.

No reason.

You're holding back on me.

Alone in the heat alone.

That's the ticket. Now we're cooking with gasoline, the Vet says.

Worried about my corpse becoming fetid in the hot air alone in my apartment.

And with that a blissful smile penetrates his face. Say no more, he says, smiling. Now I understand.

Up the stairs to her apartment. This is a bad omen, I tell myself, and that song urging me forward is a bad omen telling me how to move through this moment. I can't go through with this, I want to tell her, and just as I'm about to say, I can't go through with this, dying in the heat for a drink, my modus operandi urges me forward, telling me how to move through this moment. And so up the stairs to her apartment. She flings open the door nonchalantly. Here it is, she says, holding the door for me as I step in behind her. The hot air in her apartment is stifling but not yet fetid. Later it will be fetid. I know as I step into her apartment behind her that the hot stifling air in her apartment will one day be hot fetid air.

Have you ever smelled a corpse?

I've had enough with your corpses.

The smell of a corpse will teach you something about reality. What you like to call reality is just like your music—just like all this nonsense you listen to, pure claptrap. Stupid you should waste all of your time on this stuff. Absolutely stupid. But how would you know any better? How would you know? he asks, smiling wryly at me as if I were a child. You've never even smelled a corpse so how could you possibly know anything about music? It all stands to reason, he argues.

The air in this apartment is hot and pent up, I say to myself, stepping into her apartment as she flings open the door, but it is not fetid. One day though—and I can sense this long before that day arrives—I will step through these doors and the air will be fetid and when the air is fetid my life will be irrevocably changed. When I smell the hot fetid air of her pent-up apartment there will be a switch turned on or off and from that point on nothing will ever be the same again.

SHE FLINGS OPEN THE DOOR to her apartment, which is a wreck just like my apartment is a wreck or the Vet's apartment is a wreck, for that matter, and I can see that this gives her no pride. This is it, she says, flinging the door open and holding it for me to step in behind her. Take me as I come, she says, and with that she removes her clothes. So I take her as she comes. What other choice do I have?

But while we're at it, there's that picture of Matthew Gliss staring through his glass case at me, and when he's not staring at me there's the Technicolor tattoo on her back that is alive in a way that's almost independent of her. There is Lucy and there is Lucy's tattoo. Lucy is person A. Her tattoo is person B. Lying here with Lucy and person B is no different than lying here with Tattoo and person A. Am I making love to Lucy, I say to myself as I struggle to get used to her tattoo, or am I making love to Tattoo for her tattoo that I see, struggling to get used to it, is like a living being? It's as alive as Lucy is. There is Lucy and there is her tattoo and they are both equally alive and so who, I ask myself, grinning and bearing it as she laughs garish laughter, am I making love to here?

Who are all these dwarfs? I ask her, knowing just as certainly about the fetid smell of her apartment or about the weapon, though I don't know what kind of weapon it will be, going up the stairs to her apartment, that there are seven dwarfs now but soon, very soon, there will be eight.

These, she says, matter-of-factly, are the ones I've been with, she says, since I've been with Matthew.

How long have you been with him?

So long I can't even remember. And even if I could remember I wouldn't even tell you for it'd hurt too much to say.

I see the Technicolor tattoo, which is a magnificent work of art—the dwarfs are literally alive on her back—and as soon as I see it, as soon as she takes her clothes off—take me as I come—as soon as she removes her clothes and I see the seven dwarfs tattooed to her back, as soon as all of this transpires, I realize that I too will become a dwarf tattooed to her back—even though in my heart of hearts I suddenly, irrationally desire to be nothing less than her prince. But then I see that he's the prince staring down at me from behind his glass coffin.

Impossible to say but even as I desire more than anything to be her prince, I know—before I even think to know—that one day very soon I too will be a tattoo tattooed to her back and, like the other conquests, I too will be a dwarf. I know this as soon as she says, Take me as I come. Removes her clothes, and there, underneath her halter top, is a living work of art that features a woman who is not Snow White bending down among seven dwarfs who are not *the* Seven Dwarfs but her conquests since she's been with Matthew Gliss. I know just as soon as she removes her halter top that it's only a matter of time before I, like they, her previous conquests, am tattooed permanently to her back.

Then later, only a handful of days later, she comes up the stairs to my apartment, I open the door, and we're at it. Before we're done I see an eighth. A dwarf that looks nothing like me but that is clearly me is tattooed to her back. How is it possible, I say to myself, that there is an eighth dwarf tattooed to her back that looks absolutely nothing like me but that is nevertheless the most explicit likeness of me I have ever seen?

I have never seen an image of myself, I tell her, while she shows off what she's had done for me, more explicitly accurate than the dwarf that represents me on your back. I have never seen an image of myself that looks less like me but that is nevertheless the closest representation of myself I have ever seen, I tell her when she asks if I like it. How is it possible that this little dwarf tattooed to your back is the most uncanny representation of me I have ever seen even as I think it looks nothing like me?

It's brilliant, isn't it, she says to me, proud as hell at what she's had done to her.

Yes, it's that and more.

Look, she says, coming up the stairs to my apartment, the Vet's bum leg making a racket overhead. Look what I've done for you. I've made something permanent of you. She takes off her halter top and shows me her tattoo, which is a living breathing work of art, and newly etched to her back in Technicolor is an eighth dwarf who looks nothing like me.

He looks nothing like me, I say. But he is me.

Yes, I had to describe you to my tattoo artist. You see, he doesn't work from images, only descriptions. And so I had to describe you as meticulously as possible and as I described you he took his needle and did this to me. She smiles proudly at what she's had done.

It's brilliant, isn't it, she says to me.

Yes, it's that and more.

When I went into his shop, she says to me, I told him I wanted you on my back. So he says to me, Describe him, and I described you as meticulously as possible and with that description he did this. Isn't it wonderful?

But why? I ask.

And she says: Because it was time. I knew it was time to get more work done on my tattoo and it was natural that you should be in it. I want you close to me—don't you see? So I've added you to my tattoo. I took what money I had and I went to see my tattoo artist and I had this thing done to me. Do you like it?

It's not a matter of like, I say. It looks nothing like me but the marvel is, it is me.

I just wanted you close, so I added you on. Of course when I went to get you done Matthew stopped me on the way out and asked where I was going.

Where are you going? he asks me just as I'm about to leave. And this time I didn't tell him where I was going. I didn't tell him I was going to see my tattoo artist. I didn't tell him because if I told him who knows what might happen. Anything under the sun might happen. He might even shoot me with that stupid Glock he has if only he had half a mind to use it. Where are you going? he asks me. So I tell him: I'm going to the grocery store. I have found, living with Matthew, especially living with him since I took him back, that if I tell him I'm going to see my tattoo artist, he will freak out on me and beat the shit out of me or shoot me with that Glock of his if he has half a mind to because he can't be held responsible for what may obtain, so when I'm going to my tattoo artist I have learned to tell him the exact opposite of the truth: that I am going to pick up some groceries or something. I have found that in order to live with Matthew Gliss, which I feel I have no choice but to do, I have to tell him exactly what he wants to hear. It has occurred to me that he doesn't care if what I tell him is a lie just as long as that lie is exactly what he wants to hear. I have found that Matthew Gliss hates to hear nothing more than the truth, especially when the truth is exactly what he doesn't want to hear. So if I'm walking out the door and he asks me where I'm going, even if he knows I'm going to the tattoo artist, I am forbidden from saying: I'm going to my tattoo artist. Instead I must tell him the exact opposite of where he and I both know I'm going. Therefore, when I'm going to my tattoo artist, which we both know I'm doing, I merely have to say: I'm going to pick up a few groceries. I'll be back in several hours. OK, he'll say to me. That's fine. Don't forget to pick up some milk. But if I tell him what we both know I'm going out to do, he will beat the shit out of me because he can't be held responsible for what may obtain. And in all cases it's exactly the same. Who are all these dwarfs, he asks time to time as is his wont. Instead of telling him who all these dwarfs are, our little unspoken rule between us, which we have recently developed, is that I merely have to tell him that they are only exactly what they appear to be—nothing more nor less.

They're just dwarfs, is all, I'll say to Matthew Gliss, she'll say to me. They're just dwarfs. That's all. Nothing more nor less. *Ceci n'est pas un symbole.*

And if I say to Matthew Gliss exactly what he wants to hear—if I tell Matthew Gliss, *Ceci n'est pas un symbole,* even though it is absolutely a symbol for something else, even though both he and I both know it's a symbol for something else, even though both he and I both know exactly what it's a symbol of: the suitors I've most cherished since I've been with him. Even though he knows deep in his heart whom each and every one of these suitors is, even so—I have found that all that is required for me to say when he asks, Who are all these dwarfs? is to say that they are merely dwarfs. That's all. There's nothing more nor less tattooed to my back than dwarfs. And when I say that, he doesn't feel so bad. When I tell him something he wants to hear—that they are just dwarfs—then he has something he can hold on to, so to speak, to keep himself afloat, so to speak.

I have found, she tells me, that no one so loves to hear what they want to hear like Matthew Gliss. Especially since I've taken him back. Even if Matthew knows that what I tell him is the exact opposite of the truth, he wants to hear me tell him what he wants to hear, nothing more nor less. So that night, the night I decided to put you close to my body, I grabbed my blue bag and walked out the door, and when I stepped out the door he asked me, Where are you going? And when he asked, we both knew he knew exactly where I was going. He and I both know I only grab my blue bag when I'm going to work on my tattoo. The only time I use my blue bag is when I go to see my tattoo artist. So when I have my blue bag in hand he knows exactly where I'm going, just as he knows exactly who all these dwarfs on my back represent. Nevertheless, I tell him what he most wants to hear. That's our little unspoken rule between ourselves. You can go work on your tattoo all you want, he says to me without saying it, because it's our own unspoken rule, just as long as you don't tell me that you're going to work on your tattoo.

Tell me anything in the world you please when you are going to work on your tattoo—just don't tell me that you're going to work on your tattoo. That you're going to work on your tattoo is a truth that I for one don't care to ever hear as long as you are alive. If you ever tell me you're going to work on your tattoo, then I promise you I won't be held responsible for what may obtain. And this is exactly what happened when I chipped this tooth, she says to me. I told him, by accident, I was going to work on my tattoo and when he heard that, of course, he couldn't be held responsible for what may obtain.

Bullshit, he says, dragging me by my hair. You think you can get away with telling me this? Bullshit! Couldn't be held responsible. Who knows what the neighbors thought. Dragging me by the hair, screaming 'bullshit!' The violence of it. Mute. Slamming my face against the bathtub, then urinating on me. Mute. He actually urinated on me—can you believe that? And then two days later coming back. Forgive and forget, and that's what I did. I forgave him and we forgot, though neither of us forgot anything. Our forgetting was merely an unspoken rule never to speak the truth again, never, not as long as we live but to live with each other and always be careful to say exactly what was required to be said. Our forgetting was to forget to tell the truth, even though neither of us forgot. Even though our forgetting really was the forging of a new rule between us that we never speak the truth but always say exactly what needs to be said.

Where are you going? he asks me on the way out the door.

To get groceries, I say, carrying my blue bag, which is a signal to him that I'm going to work on my tattoo.

Don't forget to pick up a gallon of milk while you're at it.

No problem, I say.

And then: Love you, hon.

And then: Love you too, sweetie. And so that is how we've worked it out between us ever since I got this, she says, pointing to her chipped tooth, and I took him back.

But he still sees this, I point out. He still sees the tattoo and still sees you adding to your tattoo.

Yes, he sees it. But he pretends not to see it. When my skin is so sensitive from putting you close to me, when my skin is so sensitive that I'm popping pain pills like candy, he still pretends not to notice it.

Why all the pain pills? he asks.

Toothache.

You should see a dentist, he says. And by the way, get that tooth fixed while you're at it.

One day I may just do that, I say, popping pain pills like candy. When I get the cash. Anyway, tell me the truth—do you like it? she asks, coming up the stairs to my apartment. Look, she says, closing the door behind her. Look what I've had done. Do you absolutely love it? she asks.

And I know at that moment, just like I know when she slaps me at the bar. Slap slap, that this woman whom I met because her credit card wasn't working at the pump is more dedicated to me than anyone has ever been dedicated to me. And I realize, slap slap, that her dedication is a form of love, slap slap. It is the most beautiful dedication I've ever experienced, slap slap. Even though it may not be love, her dedication is sexy as hell. Even though, slap slap, it may be desperation, slap slap, sexy as hell, I say to myself, seeing the eighth dwarf taking shape on her back. Never in my life have I ever been with someone sexy as hell, and, slap slap, she smiles her mysterious smile so I take her as she comes. What other choice in all the world was there for me to make?

OF ALL THE BAD OMENS I ever overleapt, I tell the Vet.

Let me guess, he says, smoking a cigarette down to the filter so that his thumb and forefinger are yellowed with nicotine. His lips are yellowed with nicotine, as are his teeth, yellowed like old ivory, from nicotine. The Vet smokes cigarettes as if they're ventilation devices that keep him alive even though to the contrary they may end up killing him. The Vet and I sit in my kitchen listening to the Ramones, which he disparages as claptrap, or in his kitchen listening to *Die Meistersinger* or *Madama Butterfly* and always the cigarette perpetually dangles from his yellowed thumb and forefinger, his bulbous nose is occasionally singed by the burning hot coal of ash, and the walls of his apartment, like the walls of my apartment, are stained yellow by years and clouds of cigarette smoke.

These cigarettes, he'll say, time to time, are a lifeline to me. Without them, he'll say time to time, without tobacco and my music, I don't know how I could carry on with the smell of corpses in my nose.

His screen door is open and hot air from the city streets blows into his kitchen.

Please, I say, speak of cigarettes but keep your corpses out of the conversation. Time to time, I'll tell the Vet: You may speak of anything under the sun, but keep your corpses out of it for a change. No telling where things will go from there.

Have you ever smelled a corpse?

A dead one, you mean? No, and I don't intend to.

Run, don't walk.

Why is someone going to take potshots at me?

In this day and age you never know.

You smoke too much.

That's your opinion, he says.

One day you'll be a corpse, the rate you smoke, I say.

One can only hope, he says. In the meantime cigarette tobacco helps keep the smell of those corpses just a little bit at bay, he tells me, lighting a cigarette. For me, cigarettes keep the smell of corpses a little bit at bay so that's why I smoke so many of them. I smoke cigarettes, the Vet will say time to time, to keep the smell of corpses, which keep crowding in on me, at bay. A smell you never get out of your nose.

The Vet smokes as one who deeply desires suicide but who doesn't have the courage to do himself in in one fell swoop.

You smoke as if you want to die, I tell him. But you lack what it takes to do it in one fell swoop, so you're attempting death by lung cancer. That's what all this smoking amounts to.

That's what all this going to this woman amounts to for you, he says, referring to all the visits I make to Lucy, whom he calls the Tattoo Woman.

Don't call her that.

You yourself refer to her as the Tattoo Woman. You yourself have said that in a different era she'd be in a circus sideshow with her Technicolor tattoo.

But it's OK for me to call her that. She belongs to me. It's not OK for you to call her that.

Why?

It's insulting.

To whom is it insulting?

To me. And to her.

Tattoo Woman. That's what you yourself call her, and that's what I'll call her as well. Always call a spade a spade. That's my philosophy.

You and your philosophy. You don't know the half of what you think you know, I tell him.

He lets out a hilarious laugh. I suppose you do, he says, after his hilarious laugh.

Know enough to know when not to step over the line.

Bullshit, he says. You're always transgressing. You don't even know it, do you?

How always transgressing?

By telling me about my smoking, for instance. Who are you to lecture me about my smoking, when you yourself smoke?

Not only that, you see your tattoo woman for the same reason I smoke my cigarettes. You see her because you want to die.

Not true at all.

Yes, true, he says. Believe me, he says. I know a thing or two about death and truth. And you continue to see her for both reasons: curious about death, curious about truth. One day too you may get your death and truth, one day, the way you keep pursuing your tattoo woman like a hound on the trail of a bitch in heat being pulled through town on a leash by the dogcatcher. That's what this is all about. You're chasing the bitch in heat and you'll be surprised when the dogcatcher shows up to impound you.

Another time I say to the Vet, apropos of nothing in particular: You smoke because you want to die.

Just like you keep going back to that tattoo woman. Mrs. Tattoo. Who's she married to, anyway?

She's not married.

Does her whoever know you're with her?

No.

Then get out while you can. These things, let me tell you, I have a nose for these things and what you have going here is a lot worse than my cigarette smoking. It's a lot worse than your cigarette smoking too. What you have going here will only amount to no good, believe me. I have a nose for this sort of thing.

Maybe so, I say, overleaping the bad omen of it.

Maybe so, the Vet says, lighting one cigarette off the next. You should really consider taking my advice and bail on this woman. Really. You'll regret it.

Other times while talking of his corpses, the Vet will tell me: It's simple really. Some of us live longer than others. Some of us die sooner than others. Let me tell you, of all the corpses I have ever seen I have discovered that the least worthy inevitably survive. I for one am not worthy to be here and so I carry on.

Speak for yourself.

You're not worthy either to be here because if you were worthy you'd be dead right now too. Only the most worthy to live die young.

He says it again, with even greater sadness: Of all the soldiers who died with me, I may have been the least worthy to live—the least deserving—and yet I lived. You know, it's not what I intended.

What did you intend?

Not corpses. I certainly didn't intend to discover that only the most worthy for life are the first to go. That came as a complete surprise to me, and I wish that I had never learned that lesson.

Learning, I say, trying my best to console him, learning is nothing. Learning can be forgotten.

It can be remembered too. Learn your lesson from me. You never had to learn things the way I learned them. You never had to know rotted corpses except by pictures. I had to smell them rotting in the fields. And what I learned from that is that those least worthy to survive carry on while those most worthy to survive perish. It's not what I intended to discover about life. All I wanted to do was to be an artist or living in some barracks somewhere, unmolested. Instead I discovered that if you are worthy to live a long life, you will die soon. If you want to live a long life, there's no better guarantee for old age than being a scoundrel. Scoundrels live forever, I've found, and the worst scoundrels outlive everyone.

Not true, I say.

Yes, true. Do you know who dies young? Of course you don't. You didn't learn what I have learned. But you can learn from me if you want. You don't have to smell a corpse to learn from me. But if you pursue this woman—this tattoo woman—the way you're pursuing her, then one day you may smell a rotting corpse and believe you me when that day comes you will understand like you've never understood anything in your life that it was foolhardy to go this route. It was foolhardy to stick with Tattoo Woman. You will understand it was foolhardy to learn by death that only the most beautiful, the most worthy die young. The most tender and gentle souls die young. The rest of the dross—the scoundrels that is—the least worthy to live—this group always manages to live forever. They are the inheritors of the world.

TURNS THE FAN ON with her toe and begins regaling me with scenes from her life. See that picture, snapped in happier days. That's him, she says to me, flashing her mysterious smile. That's Matthew Gliss. If he ever inadvertently barges in on us, do us both a favor, don't say a word—just get up and leave as quickly as possible.

Other times she'll say: If you want to do us both a favor.

Yes?

Don't sit around looking surprised when he walks through the door. Just get up and leave. Take a good look at that picture. If you ever see someone like him walk through the door, don't waste time. Get up and go as fast as possible.

But he seems like a nice guy, I say. At least I seem to remember him being quite nice.

Nice how? she says. Drags me into the bathroom, smashes my head against the bathtub. Why? Because I'm having a work of art tattooed on my back. This tattoo that has become everything to me is everything about me that he hates. I make this tattoo not because I'm bored, not because I don't have anything better to spend my life on. I make this tattoo because he absolutely hates it. The only reason why this tattoo exists, she tells me, lighting a cigarette and passing it to me, is because I discovered that he absolutely despises tattoos. I didn't like them either, but now this tattoo is everything to me. It is the only thing, really. My life's obsession. It's not what I intended to be my life's obsession, but I happily accept it. I started out life hating tattoos, but now this tattoo is everything to me.

Whatever you do, he says to me one afternoon, eyeing me in my bikini because we were always at that damned yacht of his, whatever you do, never deface yourself like all these other women seem to be doing nowadays. Never get a tattoo. That's what he says to me: Whatever you do never get a tattoo. It was that moment, I suppose, when the idea for the tattoo was born.

How long have you known him?

So long, Robert, I've forgotten.

Or she'll say: Long enough to have this tattoo made. Long enough to spend the time needed to make this tattoo. You see this tattoo on my back?

Yes.

I started making it just after that photo behind the glass case was taken. See that photo there of the two of us on his yacht? I think it was that night that the idea for my tattoo was born. See that picture? she says, pulling it out from behind the case. Take a good look at it, she says, handing it to me. That picture captures a good deal: how happy we were at the time, because, really, we were happy. Look at his yacht. It was such a nice yacht. We had many nights of fun on that yacht. I think this picture captures that time of fun. But one thing the picture doesn't capture, she says.

What?

It doesn't capture what I'm thinking as the photo is being snapped. And this is what I'm thinking. I'll tell you what I'm thinking. I remember it as if I thought it yesterday. It was the most fateful revelation I ever had. I'm thinking, as I'm looking into the camera, that sooner or later I'm going to get a tattoo. Not a tattoo that will be small enough to hide on my ankle or ass or something but a tattoo for everyone to see. I am going to tattoo myself for everyone to see. That's what I'm thinking while the photo is being snapped. If you could look into my eyes and read my thoughts those are the thoughts you would read. I can read them now as if they were the latest headlines: I am going to get a tattoo. But you see, this picture doesn't record thoughts. It doesn't record the thought that leads to a revelation. It doesn't record the revelation that leads to a life change. I am going to get a tattoo for everyone to see—not because I like tattoos but because he absolutely despises tattoos. And even though we're smiling in that picture, truth be told, I already hate him—I hate him even as we're standing on that yacht of his smiling into the camera. I hated him on that yacht more than words can possibly say. If making a tattoo will allow me to express my hatred for him, then a tattoo it'll be. So the next day I found myself walking down Milwaukee Avenue and I stepped into the first tattoo parlor I passed. I didn't know exactly what I wanted tattooed to my back, and the particular tattoo artist I saw didn't have any set designs for me to choose from. What would you like, lady? he says to me when I step through the door. I don't know, I say. Well that's a start, he says. We can work from inspiration. That's how I work here. No preconceived designs. Come on in, he says. Sit down. You're the perfect customer and I'm just the guy you're looking for.

He proceeded to tell me how his method was to work by feel and inspiration—how the tattoo would be a collaboration between us and how this collaboration would result in a work of art that would be a pure and exact expression of who I am. So I sat down and started talking to him. We talked for weeks before he began working. He had to get to know me. We sat in coffee shops talking or in a restaurant or a bar and then one day he just began work and it was the most electrifying experience of my life. And I've been working on it now several years, and he was right, you know: This tattoo is the most intimate expression of who I am. I never thought it possible that a tattoo could be such a savior, but this tattoo has been—it's my life.

ANOTHER TIME SHE SAID vis-à-vis her tattoo: The way it happened was really random. I had no intention of getting a tattoo but I was walking down Milwaukee Avenue one afternoon past a tattoo parlor and out of curiosity, I just decided: Why not walk in and see what they have to offer? That's when I met Ronald, my tattoo artist who collaborates with me on this work. He doesn't work by photos or preset design, but he listens to me talk and while he listens he fashions this remarkable tattoo that is the most fundamentally important thing I have ever been involved in.

SHE KICKS THE FAN ON with her toe and says to me: If you for one can't handle a little risk, fine. We can part ways right now and pretend none of this ever happened. She flashes one of her mysterious smiles, which makes me proud as hell.

No, I tell her, I think I can deal with this.

Then take a good look at his picture—that one there of him standing on his yacht. Take a good look and memorize exactly what he looks like. Look at his picture and try to carry an impression away with you that will help you identify him should he ever step in on us and catch you here. Look, she says, getting up to reach for the photo behind the glass cabinet. This is him. This is Matthew Gliss and here I am. They were happier times, she says, when this photo was taken. Look—we actually look like we like each other. And look—I still have all my teeth in this picture. Look carefully here—you'll notice that Matthew has a beautiful smile. It's his most distinguished feature. He has the most beautiful smile I've ever seen. Such white teeth. In fact his smile is so beautiful I trusted it. Stupid I should have trusted it. When I first saw his beautiful smile I should have turned and run for my life. His smile is so beautiful, she tells me, holding his photo for me to see, his smile is so beautiful that when I first saw it I fell in love with it and trusted it even when I should have turned and run for my life. Smiles this perfect should never be trusted, she says, smiling one of her mysterious smiles at me. Smiles this perfect—I've come to learn the hard way that smiles as perfect as this say the exact opposite of what they say when they smile. A smiling face like this smiling face means it can't be trusted even as it says, 'trust me.' A smiling face means: 'I will destroy you because I cannot be held responsible for what obtains' even when it says, 'trust me with your life.' Seriously, such a smile says, smiling such perfect teeth, 'trust me,' even as it means the absolute opposite: 'I can't be held responsible for what obtains.' Take a good look, she says, and form an indelible image in your mind of what he looks like. Take a good look at this photo. Look at this photo until you forget you are looking at a photo—look until all you see is him. See him as he is and not as he is in this photo, if you know what I mean. Look until you forget the picture and have formed an indelible image of him in your mind. Look at the picture so carefully that the image you form of him is an image that would form of him had you actually met him and never seen a picture of him in your life. Look at it and forget it's a picture. Decide right now that what you're looking at is a real live person and you're meeting him right now in this room with me. Remember him as a real live person because one day he may walk in on us and when he does don't equivocate because you don't know who he is or because you think you can talk your way out of a confrontation with him. Recognize him immediately for who he is. Then do us both a favor: run, don't walk, and get out of here as fast as possible.

So I look at the picture of the two of them standing on board a yacht. He's in a Hawaiian shirt and she's in a white blouse and cutoffs. The city skyline is in the background and they're both smiling these incredibly beautiful smiles. Hers is beautiful without being mysterious, not because she doesn't have a mysterious smile but because it's such a fleeting mystery that I've discovered even cameras can't catch it. His smile, on the other hand, is more sinister than hers and I can see all of a sudden exactly her point. His smile is absolutely perfect and beautiful and in that perfection and beauty I sense, like she senses, something rather sinister. Who on earth has such a perfect smile, I say to myself, and is not a liar? And when no answer is forthcoming, I tell myself that his smile may be perfectly beautiful but it's also sinister precisely because of its perfection and beauty. He gazes at me from behind a pane of glass as if only a pane of glass separated him and me. I gaze back at him as if he were a he and not a photo. And before I know it he steps from the shadows of the kitchen where he's eating a slice of bread and drinking a glass of juice and lets me in.

Come on in, come in, he says. Please, sit down. Make yourself comfortable. Jeez I didn't know you were standing out there peering in on me. *Won't you come to my kitchen,* he sings in a booming voice.

So this is the man, I tell myself, as he pats me on the shoulder. This is the one I should be terrified of. It doesn't seem possible that this man, sitting so peacefully at her kitchen table, could ever do anything to harm a soul. He seems so peaceful. Impossible to believe he could ever be harmful.

I knock on her door and he gets up from the kitchen table and lets me in. The fetid smell.

Hello, I say, water water everywhere and not a drop to drink. Hot as hell today.

Are you hungry? he asks, patting my back as if we were the oldest friends in the world.

Hungry as hell.

Good, he says, flashing that beautiful smile, patting me on the back. I've breakfast ready right here for you.

When I sit down in the fetid air of her apartment I tell him, apropos of nothing, that he's my destiny. And he says: That's true only if you let me be your destiny. Of course, it doesn't have to be this way. You can go back home if you want. All you have to do, he says to me, if you don't want me to be your destiny is turn around and go back where you came from. It's that easy. Just turn around and go home. It's really not very difficult to avoid all this.

Slap slap. Sexy as hell. Just then it occurred to me that I

would never leave her, never, not as long as I or, for that matter, she lives.

You can go back to where you came from, he says, smiling his beautiful smile in the fetid air of her apartment, or sit down and have something to eat.

I'd love to, I say, taking a seat.

Come on in, then, he says. Suit yourself, he says.

So I come on in. So simple, I say to myself, crossing the threshold into the fetid air of her kitchen. Everything is so simple, this perpetual crossing of thresholds. And this, I say to myself, is what the blood ax is for. This is why we have blood axes. This is your blood ax at work, I tell myself as I cross over the threshold into her messy kitchen to have breakfast with the man with the beautiful smile who is bound to be my destiny. This is your blood ax at work, crossing the berm that naturally separated us and helping her with her card.

Hot today.

Yes.

It'll get worse, trust me. It always gets worse before it gets better.

In the end, I tell myself, it's always so simple, really. Nothing to it, really. The money is on the table, step up to it, and take it, really. That's what your blood ax is for, after all. It's to swing and use, not to have as some sort of trophy collecting dust and rust. Your blood ax is to swing, to heave-ho in the salt marsh is what it's for, I tell myself. Not to collect dust and rust like some unused useless trophy on the showroom floor.

I take a seat in the fetid air of her kitchen and I ask him: So, Matthew, tell me . . .

Yes, Robert. Wait, before you say another word, is this one of your trick questions?

Not a trick question, I say, trying to be brutally honest, just curious about something. How is it possible, I ask him even as he smiles that perfectly beautiful smile at me, that you, whom I don't even know, can loom suddenly so large in my life? We're just strangers really. What's more, you seem like a perfectly decent fellow.

Wait till you get to know me, he says, laughing as if what he just said were the funniest thing in the whole world.

You seem like a perfectly decent fellow.

That's what everyone says until they get to know me. Once you get to know me, you'll see. I can't be held responsible for what may obtain. It's just that simple.

That's nonsense, I say to him without exactly saying it.

Are you telling me it's nonsense that I can't be held responsible for what may obtain? Are you trying to tell me what I can and can't be held responsible for?

In so many words, I say to him.

Well, believe me when I say, he says to me, none of us is responsible for our actions. It's only philosophers and priests who say we're responsible for our actions. Do unto others and that kind of shit—don't believe a word of it. I don't care if we do have courts of law that send us to jail for what we've done—that still doesn't make me responsible for my actions. Entropy. That's what I believe in. Absolute entropy. Act as you please, do what you can get away with, but in the end no strings attached. Pull up a chair, he says. Make yourself comfy. I'll fix you some breakfast. How about that? Are you hungry?

Remember that time I bought you beers, I say while he fries some eggs.

Sure, never forget it, he says. You and your old buddy got

me drunk on brandies. How the hell could I ever forget? I was sick for two days afterwards.

He smiles at me. His smile is gorgeous and full of beautiful white teeth. When he smiles I somehow feel as if all of this were déjà vu, or déjà vu's opposite—that I'm seeing something before it happens.

I've been here before, I tell him, meaning: I'll be here again. I can feel it in my bones that even though this is not happening it will happen in the fetid air of her kitchen.

Of course you have, he says. Of course you will, he says. That explains why I'm going to be your destiny. If you didn't want for me to be your destiny, he says to me in all seriousness, you would have never agreed to go home with her in the first place. You would not have even helped her gas up her car. If you didn't want me to become your destiny, he says to me in all seriousness, then you very simply would have declined her offer at the gas station and gone on home. You would have left while you still had a chance.

I feel as if I've done this before with you, even though we've never done this before, and that we'll do it again even though we're not even doing it right now, I say to him.

It does seem vaguely familiar, doesn't it? he says. Here, have an egg.

And while I eat my egg, he asks again: You said déjà vu. Is eating the egg part of the déjà vu experience?

I take a sip of orange juice and try to answer his question.

Not the egg, I say after a moment, because, frankly, eating the egg doesn't at all seem familiar. What seems familiar, however, is drinking the orange juice and eating the bread in the fetid air. That's the déjà vu part. And the weapon.

What's familiar, I tell him, as far as I can tell, is just sitting here with you drinking orange juice and eating a slice of bread in the fetid air.

He pulls out a knife and starts cutting a slice of bread from a huge loaf. Would you like a piece?

Sure, I say. Why not?

Her kitchen, like the Vet's kitchen, opens up to a back porch and the door is open so hot air from the streets blows into her apartment but doesn't blow the hot fetid smell away.

If I ever catch you with her, he says, apropos of nothing, I can't be held responsible.

That's ridiculous, I tell him. Of course you'll be held responsible.

I'm just telling you right now if I ever catch you with her, he takes a drink from his orange juice and deliberately sets his glass on the table, I'll have no compunction about killing you. Do you understand?

How can you sit there and say that? I ask him. How can you threaten to kill me while drinking an orange juice on such a beautiful morning?

I'm just warning you: I can't be held responsible.

I climb the stairs to her apartment and there he is. I see him through the window eating a piece of bread and drinking a glass of orange juice. So this is him, I tell myself, trying to get as good a look at him as possible—which is what she advises I do if I'm going to accept this risk. I look him over. If I'm going to accept this risk, I say to myself, doing nothing in half measures, I better memorize him from head to toe. So this is the guy, who, catching me in bed with Lucy, this is the guy who will separate me from my life or vice versa, I think to myself—and as soon as I think that vice versa I'm suddenly overcome with grief. We die of broken hearts, the Vet says to me one day, listening to *Die Meistersinger* and talking of the horrors of war. And broken bankbooks, he says to me one day at the track, the way we're going. He's the guy who will separate me from my life or vice versa, I think to myself, overcome with grief, for I wouldn't own one even if I could.

He's the one, I tell myself, to watch out for. He's the one with the Glock—I wouldn't own one even if I could. He's the one to shoot his Glock or some such thing and not be held responsible for what obtains or vice versa.

Tell me this, I ask him one day, apropos of nothing.

Is this a trick question?

You seem like a nice guy.

Wait till you get to know me, he says, smiling. And I can tell by the way he smiles that he knows what he refuses to let himself know: that all the dwarfs tattooed on her back are suitors whom she's been with as far back as they've been together.

How is it that it will come to pass?

It doesn't have to be this way. You can turn around, go back where you came from.

Don't you realize I have to hold you responsible?

Nonsense. No such thing as being held responsible. Don't believe a word of it. That being held responsible is voodoo magic whipped up by priests and philosophers. Cut yourself a little slack and forget about such nonsense. No need whatsoever to be held or hold someone responsible.

I feel my life . . . , I tell the Vet.

Yes?

I feel my life has become . . .

What are you trying to say?

And when I don't have the courage to put it into words he gets up and switches his tape. Here, sit back. Listen to this, he says, will you. And so we listen, and periodically he chimes in with: The beauty, the beauty.

I DON'T HAVE A PICTURE OF YOU, she says one day, smiling her mysterious smile, which, I admit to myself, is more beautiful and mysterious than I ever remember it being. She, like Epstein, is continually surprising me. When I think she can't be any more mysterious than she already is, she shows up at the bar to visit me and she's more mysterious than ever. Just when I think Epstein has no more secrets, he proves he has another one up his sleeve, out fishing by the river in the virgin wilderness becoming one with all the animate and inanimate creatures of the world. The essence of mystery, I'm beginning to realize, is that it's really just the capacity for endlessly emerging secrets.

Mystery, I tell the Vet one day, sitting at the fireplace in the bar because a stranger is tending the bar, mystery is just a capacity for revealing endlessly emerging secrets.

Sounds like bullshit to me.

Well then what the hell do you think mystery is?

I don't believe in it at all, the Vet says. I've seen too much in my day to believe in mystery. I think, he says to me, being brutally honest, that mystery is a total crock of bull. It's a crock of shit is what it is. A crock of bullshit, if you know what I mean.

How about your music? I point out. Surely you must think *Die Meistersinger* or *Madama Butterfly* mysterious.

Not mysterious, just music, he says. Neither of these pieces of music is mysterious. They're just musical pieces is what they are, he says. You have to see things for what they are, you see, he says. And anything that conceals—any person who conceals in an attempt to be mysterious—is a crock of shit.

I disagree.

Of course you disagree, the Vet says to me. You live a life enthralled by those things that conceal. You are afraid to step out of your apartment on a hot day, for Christ's sake, because of the light from the sun. Mystery doesn't live in the light of day; it likes the dark. Mystery can't handle the light of day, always sitting in the shadows. But what I think about all of this is it's a crock of shit.

What about your artwork? I say, pointing to his famous picture book.

My artwork is just a bunch of photos of derelict bikes, is all. It is nothing more nor less, he says. I'm not attempting to say anything mysterious at all, he says. Only trying to show what's out there in the light of day beneath our very noses. What you'll see, he says to me, lighting a cigarette after I return from my jukebox, having fed a five-dollar bill into it, what you'll see, he says to me, lighting his cigarette, is that if you ever get to the bottom of what's actually being concealed by mystery, what you'll actually find there is nothing but a bunch of abandoned and derelict bicycles attached by chain or hook to fence, post, or tree. That's all. All mystery ever conceals, he says to me, is the everydayness of the every day. All mystery is, he says to me, it's all a big show to hide the obvious—that the tall man is really a small man at heart, the strong man a weak man, etcetera, etcetera.

But beauty, I say. Your beauty. The beauty you experience every time you listen to your music. Beauty is a mystery.

You're wrong there too, the Vet says, lighting one cigarette off the other. Beauty is just an emotion. No different, really, than joy. No different, really, even than love.

WHO ARE ALL THESE DWARFS? I ask her one day. We're lying in bed boiling in the heat. She kicks the fan to life with her toe.

Stupid question, she says.

Who are all these dwarfs?

Look, she says, pointing to the outlined figure of an eighth dwarf. I'm putting you here too, she says, pointing to the outline of an eighth dwarf. Look at this dwarf, she says, pointing to the outline of a dwarf on her back. Well what do you think of it? she asks. How do you like yourself in my tattoo? Isn't it beautiful?

Who is it supposed to be? I ask, pointing to the eighth dwarf.

You, of course, she says. Can't you see?

Who are all these dwarfs?

My suitors, she says. You asked; I answered. Are you happy?

Listening to her talk of her suitors is like listening to the Vet tell about corpses. I'd sooner listen to you tell me anything than hear you tell about corpses.

I'd sooner hear you talk about the weather than listen about all the others, I tell her.

Be careful what you ask then, she says, if you don't want to know. Don't ask. It's as simple as that.

Tell me this, I ask.

Shoot.

What would you do if you—believing your fiancée to be faithful—discovered her one day in bed with another guy?

Why is my fiancée doing something behind my back that I don't know about?

It's a theoretical question, is all, I tell him.

Cut it with the bullshit. Is she doing something behind my back that I don't know about?

No, but she's doing something behind her back.

Who are all these dwarfs tattooed to your back?

Do you really want to know the answer?

I suppose not.

Then be careful what you ask for—you just might get it.

If I caught my fiancée in bed with another guy, I've already told her I won't be held responsible for what may obtain. From that point forward I would say everything and anything would be in play. Who the hell knows. I might even . . .

Run, don't walk, and hide.

Why? Is someone going to start taking potshots at me?

In this world, you never know, but if they do, do yourself a favor: Run, don't walk, and hide.

If he ever walks through the door and sees you here . . .

Yes?

Do yourself a favor: Run, don't walk, and hide. He has a Glock and the damage that thing can do is incredible. Believe me when I say he won't be afraid to use it on you or me for that matter.

Are you trying to tell me he'll kill me if he catches me here?

All I'm saying is what he told me. He tells me he can't be held responsible for what may obtain if he catches you or anyone else like you here.

That's ridiculous, I point out. Of course he can be held responsible for his actions—that's what courts of law are for.

Be sure to mention that to him, she says, laughing as if I were the funniest thing she's ever met, when he's pointing that Glock at you.

All of a sudden I'm irrationally terrified. It terrifies me to be here with a woman who has a man who will think nothing of killing me if he catches me. This isn't what I intended, I tell myself. Have I suddenly stepped into a hornet's nest?

If you can't handle the risk, she says, smiling at me as I walk down the stairs from her apartment, I won't blame you for walking away and never coming back. She flashes her smile, which is filled with mystery and makes me, suddenly, proud as hell. Just then my modus operandi kicks in. No need to worry about that, I tell her, trying to reflect her smile back at her with one of my own. I won't do anything in half measures with you. I'll always be all or nothing.

Good, because I've had a lovely time and I'd love for you to come back.

It only takes a piece of lead moving at a few hundred miles an hour to separate you from the living, the Vet tells me. Just the tiniest piece of lead is all that it takes. Don't you see? the Vet points out. We're really very delicately rigged. It doesn't take that much to mess this up.

When I get back to my place the Vet is waiting for me. Why'd you do it? he asks.

It was easy as pie, is all.

That's not it.

Hot as hell. She offered me a drink.

Getting closer.

I didn't want to be alone in my hot apartment.

That's it, he says, slapping me on the back. That's the ticket. Now we're cooking with gasoline.

Later at the dump, plinking away, telling me all about it: Beautiful piece of mechanicals, these Glocks here.

Or when I ask him, What are you doing to effect immortality? he laughs because he doesn't mean it. Not a damned thing and it's killing me, he says.

WHERE YOU GOING? the Vet asks as I step out the door that fateful day.

Gas up my car I suppose, I say.

About time, he says. I was going to offer to do it for you. I hated to see that car just rot on the curb, collecting parking tickets because you never got around to gassing it up.

I'm going to put air in the tires too I suppose, I say to the Vet as I close the door behind me and descend the two flights of stairs to the street. Be back in a few minutes.

And get it washed while you're at it, he shouts after me.

We'll see about that, I say, and with that I'm off. I step outside and I'm shocked by what a blast furnace it is out of doors in the blazing heat. All summer long sitting in my apartment watching news reports of all the people dropping dead of heatstroke. Never before have so many infirm and elderly died in their apartments alone in the heat of heatstroke and dehydration. Never before has the city morgue been so filled to overflowing with the John and Jane Doe corpses of so many lonely people dead of heatstroke, dehydration, and neglect. It's neglect as much as anything that's killing all these John and Jane Doe people alone in the heat, I thought to myself. The reason why all of these John and Jane Doe people are dying is not merely because they are dehydrated in the heat but because they are neglected in their apartments, alone in the heat. And being neglected too long in your apartment alone is the same as being deeply dehydrated, only it's more fatal than dehydration. One of the problems, I have found, with living alone is that if you live too long alone in your apartment people stop checking in on you time to time to see how you're doing. One of the worst things about living alone too long by yourself is that people begin to take you for granted living alone by yourself and they stop checking in on you to see how you're doing and this type of neglect, too much of it, can be more fatally dangerous than actual dehydration.

Neglect, I tell the Vet, is probably tantamount to dehydration, only worse.

Probably true, he says to me. By the way that Glock you inquired about—

Yes?

I'll have it for you in a day or so.

I step onto the street to gas up my car in the blast furnace and I curse my luck that I live alone neglected in my apartment during such a brutal heat wave when in actuality I started out life with the best of intentions. My intentions when I started out in this life were not to live alone in my hot apartment like the Vet lives alone in his hot apartment or countless John and Jane Does live alone in their hot apartments but to live like Epstein lives who lives in a house with a beautiful family: a wife—his childhood sweetheart, Meg—and two kids, lovely kids really. Just wonderful, lovely beautiful kids really. And it's true that it's always been my intention to live in a house with a sweetheart and children even before I knew there was an Epstein whom I could emulate. Before there was an Epstein whom I could emulate I carried with me a vague notion of what I wanted out of life. I never knew exactly what I wanted, but I knew more or less exactly what I didn't want and what I didn't want most of all was to live alone in an apartment like so many Jane and John Does living alone in their hot apartments, living their neglected and anonymous lives alone. Of all the things in the world that I wanted to do the thing that I absolutely least wanted to do was to live alone in my apartment like a John or a Jane Doe. That was top on my list of things I absolutely never wanted to do. What I really wanted to do with my life was more difficult to say. Nevertheless I felt that *want* like a premonition. The *want* in my life was like a premonition even though I could never quite put my finger on what exactly that *want* was.

What do you want out of life? the Vet would ask time to time, seeing my blood ax collecting dust and rust in the corner of my one-bedroom dump.

Hard to say, I would tell the Vet. Hard to put into words exactly what I want, but I know I want something. I distinctly know I want something though as yet I am unable to put a finger on it. I know this, I would tell the Vet whenever he raised the issue of want: I know I can't put my finger on what I want. At the same time, though, I feel what I want as if it were some sort of premonition or wishing well in my apartment urging me to leap into it.

It went on this way for years. Such vague premonitions. Then I met Epstein, my Mystic, and everything changed. All of a sudden I started to have a better idea of what I wanted, though once I could say exactly what I wanted, I found that it was still nearly impossible for me to put into words how exactly I would go about getting what I wanted. It's one thing to want something, I realized, and another thing to go about getting what you want. It's one thing to say I want X but it's another thing altogether to actually put a plan together that will practicably allow one to obtain X.

It was only after I met Epstein my Mystic that I realized he represented for me an ideal of something. The life he was living and the way he was living it—I thought that I should try to emulate it somehow. There were several aspects of Epstein my Mystic that I thought worth emulating. His mysticism, for instance, was worth emulating and the thing about Epstein's mysticism was that it represented one of the most beautiful stances to the world that I have ever seen a person take. In all of my life I have never met a person like Epstein who takes what I can only call a mystical approach to living his life. Epstein is a man who, unlike most people I've ever met, is absolutely at peace with himself in the world. If Epstein were like me, alone in his apartment, it would be an eminently tenable situation for him. He is such a mystical person, so filled with a oneness and love and acceptance for all the animate and inanimate creatures of the world in a sacred unity, that it didn't seem to matter to him, really, whether he was head of a beautiful household or alone in some crappy apartment in the heat. It occurred to me that the one good thing about Epstein's mysticism is that it inured him to the plight of being alone. In fact being alone was probably the one thing Epstein most excelled at. If you had to be alone, then the best way to be alone, it occurred to me, especially after I had come to know Epstein, is to be like Epstein, a mystic alone with all the animate and inanimate creatures in a sacred unity. The thing about mystics, I thought to myself after having come to know Epstein, who himself is a natural mystic, is that they are inured to loneliness. In fact mystics craved loneliness. The reason why Epstein turns into a stone fishing by the river in our virginal wilderness while I natter on about my life, trying to catch a carp, is because Epstein for one thing is not concerned with appearances. Nor is he troubled by being absolutely completely alone. He can be the most alone person I have ever met—alone but unified with all things animate and inanimate in a sacred unity. He is alone even when he's surrounded by his family making such beautiful noises in the morning when he calls every third day to check in on me. The advantage that someone like Epstein my Mystic has in life is that he is entirely suited to the condition of aloneness, whereas I am a person—no matter how much I try to emulate Epstein by sitting on my perfect park bench trying to become a stone—who finds it acutely painful to be alone in my apartment in the heat living my anonymous life alone. I also find it extremely hard to become, like Epstein, a stone. I hate being alone—even though in my heart of hearts I wish I could be alone like Epstein is alone. I hate being in my apartment alone. There is nothing more painful to me than the realization that I have become what I least wanted to become out of life. What I really wanted to become out of life was someone like Epstein. I wanted to become someone like Epstein before I even knew an Epstein existed. Epstein helped me see that becoming an Epstein was exactly what I wanted to become: a mystic at peace with being alone. On the one hand, I came rather quickly to realize that what comes easily for Epstein doesn't come so easily for me. Unlike Epstein, no matter how much I try, I am unable to become a stone. Unlike Epstein, no matter how much I try, I am unable to become a family man. I would be happy if I could be a mystic. I would be elated if I could be a family man, yet try though I might to be either a mystic or a family man I have found that I have become, contrary to everything I had ever hoped for in the world, a lonely person alone in my hot apartment.

Though I truly wish to become like Epstein, the exact opposite has actually happened: I have become exactly like the Vet. I wanted one thing—to become like Epstein—and got another—I became like the Vet. I have tried everything in my powers to do everything possible not to become exactly like the Vet, and yet, when it's all said and done, there's no one whom I more closely resemble than the Vet. Although I don't have the carbuncles and welts from acne that the Vet has, yet I have become incredibly similar to the Vet. There's no way to describe how I went from wanting to be like Epstein but ended up being like the Vet—lonely and alone—other than to say my life is truly out of my control. The direction of my life seems to be out of my hands. I can no sooner control my life than I can control the life of the guy down the street who sits on his front porch drinking beer out of a paper bag all day long, cursing at the people who walk by. Try though I might to steer my life in Epstein's life direction, I find that my life inevitably steers itself—against my will—into the Vet's life direction. Instead of becoming a decent upright citizen, which is what I had intended, I have become, to the contrary, a sort of monster. Instead of becoming like Epstein, a decent upright citizen, I have become, like the Vet, a monster of sorts. Try though I might to emulate Epstein, I can't escape the feeling that I, like the Vet, am marginalized in my apartment alone, an absolute outsider in my apartment alone.

Do you realize—I say to the Vet one brutally hot night, walking down the unremittingly hot street when a stranger coming our way switches over to the other side of the street to keep clear of us—do you realize, I point out to the Vet, what absolute outsiders we are? It was funny that we never realized what outsiders we were until we encountered a stranger who, thinking we were dangerous or unruly or trouble, crossed over to the other side of the street. And now I see it wasn't so unnatural that a stranger should be afraid of us. We each live in one-bedroom apartments and both of our apartments are disaster zones. Occasionally, I would go to the Vet's apartment and he'd have a broom in hand, or he'd have a mop in hand, and he'd set about cleaning the place. After he cleaned his place he would urge me to clean mine. When he came down to my place for drinks after having just cleaned his place, he would be brutally honest with me and tell me he thought my place was a dump.

This place you have here is a dump. You shouldn't live like an animal. There's no need for it. You ought to spend a little of your time and clean it up.

I'd put some music on, like "The KKK Took My Baby Away," which is only my second or third favorite song in the whole world.

And he would say: What is this nonsense?

And I'd say: "The KKK Took My Baby Away."

It's an insult, he'd say, to the KKK.

Madama Butterfly is an insult, I would say, trying to be brutally honest, to your so-called Orientals.

That's an insult to me.

Well, what about all your comments against the Ramones—you calling them claptrap?

Because that's what they are—claptrap.

We talk a bunch of nonsense.

That we do.

It's what I love about our friendship.

Say, did you see the way the stranger at the bar was avoiding us today? As if we were a couple of mongrels.

We are mongrels, I'd point out. What the hell do you think we are? People in the real world think we're nuts. It's only luck that keeps us out of prison.

And our good looks, the Vet would say.

Speak for myself, I would tell him.

I am. And I agree with you. Only luck keeps us out of prison. And it shouldn't be that way. Do you realize what I have given to this country of mine? Do you have any idea what sort of sacrifice I have made for this country of yours and now you're telling me it's only luck that's keeping us from getting locked up?

Apropos of nothing the Vet slammed his fist through the wall, breaking a knuckle.

Do you have any idea what sacrifices I have made and you're telling me they think we're a bunch of freaks? I'm a fucking American. What the hell more do I need to do to prove that? Smash, hand through the wall, broken knuckle. Screaming ensues. Crying both rational and irrational follows. I make him an ice bucket. Here, I say. Meanwhile *Die Meistersinger* plays on his cassette player.

He gets up from where he's sitting. Reaches in his drawer. Here, take this, he tells me, setting the Glock on the table. Take this with you. You asked for it—now you have it.

I hug him. I don't know why I hug him, perhaps because at times it seems he's all I've got. Perhaps I hug him because, like it or not, he's all I really have in the world. Of everyone in this world I have ever loved no one has stuck by me through thick and thin like the Vet. The Vet understands better than anyone my life trajectory because he, more than anyone, has already lived a life that has made the same trajectory my life is now making. His life trajectory pattern—alone in his hot apartment—is the same life trajectory as mine—only he's at a higher end of the arc because he's been living his life trajectory longer than I've been living mine.

We have the same paths, I would tell him time to time.

That we do.

Only you're further along the path than I am.

With a little patience though, he would say to me ever so sweetly, you'll catch up in no time.

You're like a brother to me, I tell him.

Get off that shit, he tells me. None of this maudlin shit between us. Only the brutal truth. OK?

Well, here's the brutal truth, I tell him.

Go home. Take your gun. Good night. I'll call you in the morning.

I SUPPOSE I WAS FEELING deeply neglected that blazing hot summer day as well as dehydrated and perhaps that's why, sitting alone on the couch, I decided, apropos of nothing, to go gas up my car at the nearest station. Why else would I have gassed my car up on one of the hottest days on record? Looking back, I can honestly say I had hoped that things would have turned out differently but this is my life, I tell myself, turning the ignition on to my AMC Hornet and very carefully driving it down the street to the nearest gas station. And my life is like the Vet's life, I tell myself, starting up the ignition to my car. He may be twenty-five years older than me, but still, I'm very nearly exactly like the Vet. In reality, it's no understatement to say I had hoped I would have been married or something by now—me a twenty-eight-year-old man with no real plans to speak of. I had hoped that by now I would have had my life in order but my life, like my apartment and the Vet's apartment for that matter, was completely and absolutely disheveled. Three days after the Vet's cleaning jag, I knew as a matter of absolute fact that it would only take a few days and his life would descend back into chaos. It will only take a few days, I remember telling myself whenever I would go up to his apartment and see him with his broom in hand, it will only take a few days before his life and his apartment for that matter descend back into chaos. The chaos is too great for someone like the Vet to keep at bay. The chaos is too great even for someone like me, for that matter, to resist. What's more, it's always been my only dream to be able to resist the chaos and yet sooner or later I always succumb to the chaos of doing nothing. Entropy, for me I have found, has been the most natural state in the world. Between doing something or nothing, I have always chosen to do nothing. Between establishing order or sinking into chaos, I invariably have always let myself sink into chaos. I don't choose chaos because I desire chaos, I see now. I choose chaos because of all things in the world chaos is the state I'm least able to resist. As a result my blood ax collects dust and rust because it's unwilling to do anything other than collect dust and rust, watching the day turn to night, watching all of the seasons pass by.

This place you have here is a dump. You shouldn't live like an animal, the Vet says, being brutally honest. There's no need for it. No need to live like this. You ought to spend a little of your time and clean it up. Sweep the floors, scrub your tub, lift the shades—let a little light into this dump. It doesn't need to be like this after all.

I'd put on some music like "The KKK Took My Baby Away," or even, in a rare mood, *Billion Dollar Babies* by Alice Cooper, which I love for reasons I can't quite put my finger on even though, in reality, it is quite a silly album.

It's only a matter of hours, I would tell the Vet, being absolutely brutally honest with him, before you go back to living like a slob. Believe me, I would tell him if he pushed the issue after one of his cleaning jags when he attempted to surmount the disorder that was everywhere coming down upon him, it's only a matter of days before you slip back into your old ways—before your filthy habits take hold once again. It won't take long now, I would say to the Vet after he hung up his broom and dustpan in the coat closet, before you slip into your old messy ways. And it was true. I was right. It never took the Vet but a couple of days before he was right back where he'd started—always misplacing his cassettes in a pile of junk, trash, and debris that kept growing like an excrescence on every available surface in his apartment. Cigarette ashtrays were scattered everywhere in his apartment. His walls were yellowed by years of smoke.

This is an execration, I would say, going up to his apartment three or four days after his cleaning jag. I thought you could hold the debris at bay but apparently not, I would tell the Vet. Walking into the Vet's apartment and seeing what a wreck his place was, I would gently point out that the filth in his place was an absolute excrescence. Unbelievable, I would point out—bugs and cockroaches everywhere. Who are you to lecture me? I would point out. Who are you to say anything about how I live when you live like this, like an absolute pig—this excrescence.

At least I tried, he would say. There's something to be said for trying, he would say. At least I tried to clean my place. Isn't that better than you who doesn't even try?

NEVER MEANT FOR MY LIFE to be like this in the first place. Never meant to live like this in an apartment, such a wreck. Never meant to live like the Vet lives. I had always intended for more but somehow have never been able to obtain more. How is it, I would ask myself, coming home from the river after carp fishing with Epstein, that Epstein has been able to figure out how to get his life in order but I have absolutely failed to figure out how to get my own life in order? How is it Epstein makes getting one's life in order seem so effortless and seamless when it has been the most difficult challenge imaginable for me to obtain order?

I never thought getting my life in order would be such an insurmountable challenge, I would tell Epstein time to time driving in his car to or from the river. Sitting on the muddy riverbank surrounded by massive green leafy trees and the sounds of insects churring, I never thought getting my life in order would prove so impossible, but in truth it really has been gruelingly impossible, I would tell him.

You should get out more, Epstein would say, offering blessedly helpful words of advice.

Again, I would point out: This is all easy for you to say. You've already accomplished everything you need to accomplish, but for me it's not so easy.

And he would say: But, yes, it is. It is easy. You just have to go do it, that's all. It's all in the doing, he would say. That's all. Nothing to it, really. Just go out there and do whatever it is you wish to do.

And in truth Epstein is right as usual even though I find it hard to admit while talking to him that as usual he's right and I'm wrong. As in everything else, Epstein has proved once again that he's more often right than I am. Epstein's judgment, unlike mine, always proves to be infallible. Even while fishing on the bank of the river, fishing in our virginal wilderness under a canopy of trees in one of the loveliest spots along the river for carp, even then Epstein's judgment is impeccable. Got one, I would say, watching my rod tip bob, but Epstein always could tell the difference the river makes on a rod tip bobbing from how an actual fish makes the rod tip bob. I think I have one, I would tell Epstein, reaching for my rod.

I don't think that's a fish, Epstein would say. It's only the river. And he'd be right. Epstein was much better than I at reading a bobbing rod tip. If it jerks sharply, he would say, then it's a carp nibbling at the bait. If it jerks softly it's only the current trying to take the bait downriver.

May I confess something to you? I would ask when the moment seemed propitious.

Go ahead.

I feel my life has become uselessly aimless.

You should get out more often.

Good idea, I say, for he is absolutely right even though I find it hard to admit that he's right and I'm wrong. Who am I, after all, to complain about my life? What right do I have, after all, to confess to Epstein, of all people, that my life isn't what I intended it to be? And so there we are fishing alongside the river and I'm nattering on about my life, such as it is, while Epstein, lulled by the soft bobbing of the rod tip becomes, for a while, a stone.

My life has become absolutely unnatural to me, I tell myself, getting in the car to take it to the gas station. My life has become absolutely unnatural to me because I feel as if it's out of my control. When I want my life to go one way, it veers the exact opposite direction. When I want to become like Epstein, I become, against my best wishes, exactly like the Vet—an absolute outsider, alone in my hot apartment. I have no idea what may become of me, I keep telling myself, living alone in my blazing hot apartment. And if something should happen to me, who would be there to help other than the Vet or Epstein? I love both the Vet and Epstein, love them each like brothers, but at the end of the day, I don't love them enough to entrust my life to them.

Hey, Robert, where you going? the Vet asks as I step out of my apartment.

Just down the block to gas up my car. Back in a minute.

Come on up for a beer when you get back.

I drive very carefully down the street, careful not to accelerate too quickly lest I cause the car to burn more gas than necessary. I'm running on fumes, really, I tell myself as I drive carefully to the nearest gas station. Be careful, I tell myself, not to accelerate too quickly lest you suddenly use up the last of your fuel reserves. I'm running on fumes. Terrible situation to be running on fumes on such a brutally hot day. I should have planned to keep more gasoline in my car so as not to be in this desperate situation. If I had more gas in my car than just fumes, who knows, perhaps I would have gotten gas at the edge of town where it's always cheaper. Had I gotten gas at the edge of town where it's always cheaper none of this ever would have happened.

The reason why this has happened, I tell myself as I withdraw and roll over to my side of the bed sweating in the heat, is simple. I had run out of gas and so driving on fumes

I had to pick the nearest gas station in town. Had I picked any other gas station in town, none of this ever would have happened, I tell myself as I withdraw and roll over to my side of the mattress.

She clicks the fan on with her toe, then lying next to me begins stroking my calf with her foot.

See that picture over there, she asks me, on the dresser? That's him. That's my fiancé. I can't believe I'm calling him *my* fiancé. It should have never proceeded this far. I should never have been with him so long that he would corner me into getting engaged to him.

When are you guys scheduled to get married? I ask.

We aren't. He keeps asking me for a date and I stall him. I want to stall him as long as possible. I want to stall him because of all the people in the universe, he's the one I *least* want to marry. Marrying him would be an absolute disaster. Marrying him would be a death sentence, just like I'm almost certain that being his fiancée is also a certain death sentence. If it's a death sentence either way then why the hell bother with the wedding? That's what she asks me: Why the hell bother with the wedding? Just then he does what we least expect him to do at the absolutely least propitious moment imaginable. He walks in on us.

One more, I say, lighting up a cigarette.

Sure.

He walks in on us.

Is that him? I distinctly remember asking.

Well it's not Santa Claus and it's not Jesus Christ. That only leaves one other person who might barge in on us unannounced.

Theoretically, I say, what would you do?

Take the money and run. That is, if the bills were untraceable.

Let me ask you a question.

Is this a joke?

No, a theoretical question: In theory, what would you do?

My fiancée going behind my back with someone else? I'd probably kill the bastard, though no guarantees.

One more, I say, lighting up a cigarette.

She clicks the fan on with her toe and he walks in on us.

Matthew, she says.

What's going on here?

What do you mean?

I get up and run like hell.

You think you can do this behind my back? Plink. I hear him scream as I run all the way down the stairs to my AMC Hornet.

WHO KNOWS WHAT THE NEIGHBORS THINK, she tells me one day apropos of her tattoo, with him shouting 'bullshit' at the top of his lungs. Hated him so long I can't even say. Hated him so long I wouldn't say even if I could for fear of embarrassment. Know him—how? If you knew him like I know him you would see that no one ever buys someone like Matthew Gliss drinks. Take a good look, she says. Look as if it's not a picture you're looking at but a person. Look and memorize him as a true flesh-and-life person. See—that's us in happier days. I still have all my teeth. If you ever see him walk in on us, do us both a favor, Robert: Don't equivocate, just run like hell and save yourself. Don't worry a thing about me. I for one can handle anything he has to give and I'm prepared to do so.

I SWIM AT THE BOTTOM of the well waiting for her to call when, apropos of nothing, she calls.

Tell me, she says when I pick up the phone.

Yes.

Why'd you come home with me today?

I don't know.

Is it love that made you come?

I don't know.

Is that what this is about? she asks me, speaking quietly into the phone. Love?

It's about the heat is what it is, I tell her to the best of my ability.

You were watching me pump my car with gas—I saw you. You were watching me.

No I wasn't.

Yes, you were.

Maybe. Why'd you help me?

You asked.

I didn't ask.

Did too.

See, there you go again, putting thoughts into my head.

I never once put a thought into your head.

It was your idea to come to my place today. I merely made it easy for you and invited you.

LYING ON MY COUCH in the insufferable heat, listening to reports on the radio of the dead. How they're mounting up. Never before have so many died so alone in the heat. Never before have the morgues filled to capacity with John and Jane Does dead of neglect, which is worse than heat and dehydration.

I sit in my hot fetid apartment alone waiting for her to call. My gun sits in the bottom drawer in the hot fetid apartment. I sit waiting for the call. When will she call? I ask myself. I'm careful not to fall into a tube-watching cycle. I sit with my blood ax collecting dust and rust in the corner, watching the light change from dawn to morning to dusk to night, watching the weather, which is unrelentingly hot and fetid. I wake myself in the middle of the night. Before I met her I awoke interested only in seeing that I was still breathing. Now I awake feeling her absence, which ramifies my sense of aloneness. I am too much alone in my apartment, I tell myself when I awake in the middle of the night, to see if I am still among the living or if I have passed into the land of the unknown, the land of the dead. I stir and my eyes open wide. A moment to collect my bearings. I'm alive, still among the living. Keep staying alive among the living, living alone in my hot apartment, waiting for a call that will never come.

I STEP OUTSIDE MY APARTMENT into the blazing sun to locate my car on the street. The sun is blazing hot—a blast furnace really. When I step out of my apartment building to locate my car I am physically struck by the heat as if it were a battering ax. It's a blast furnace and when I step out into it from my apartment I am nearly knocked down instantaneously. I step outside of my apartment building and I'm almost immediately knocked down instantaneously from the brutally hot force of the blazing sun. My eyes are blinded by the light, having stepped out of my dark apartment where I have lain on my couch in front of the tube so many days, caught in a vicious tube-watching cycle, water water everywhere, I didn't know what to do. It takes several minutes in the blazing heat and blinding sun before my eyes can adjust to the radically extreme conditions of the hot air rising off the concrete sidewalk like a sledgehammer nailing me square in the eyes. This is not a good idea, I distinctly remember saying to myself as I step into the cruel unremitting heat struggling for breath. Surely this is a terrible idea to be stepping out into this heat at midday on such a brutally hot day, and off I go overlooking yet another bad omen. So many dead alone in their hot fetid apartments alone.

And who is going to look in on us time to time? the Vet asks. For if I die and you die on the same night then our corpses will go undiscovered.

Brilliant observation, I say.

Cut it with that shit. We can't go on forever only looking after ourselves. Someone needs to look in on us—a third party.

It's neglect more than anything that's killing all of these John and Jane Does. Neglect is worse than dehydration. Neglect is worse than heat and dehydration. Neglect is the worst.

We need a third party, the Vet points out. We can't just rely on ourselves. This is not a sufficient safeguard.

And so I go up the steps to her apartment. I climb the steps, Glock in hand, the derelict swimming pool a bad omen, which I overleap. It's a bad omen and I acknowledge that the pool and the apartment in such derelict condition are both bad signs yet I keep climbing because I've been swimming so long and when I finally reach her apartment I stare in through the window and see that he's sitting alone at her kitchen table—which, like the Vet's kitchen table, and my kitchen table for that matter, is a mess, crowded and overcome with dirty dishes and empty boxes and debris and filth.

I look in through the window and he just sits there calm, inviolate among the debris at the table, eating a piece of bread and drinking a glass of orange juice in the fetid air. He's shorter than I remember him but then again I only see him in shadows. He's in the shadows of her kitchen, which is filth, eating a slice of bread and drinking a glass of orange juice. He sits alone amid the filth of her kitchen, inviolate, self-absorbed, eating a slice of bread and drinking his orange juice in the fetid air. And I see, watching him in the shadows of her kitchen, that he is just a man eating a slice of bread and drinking a glass of orange juice, is all. Of all the things in the world he could be right now, I say to myself, he is only this: a man eating a piece of bread and drinking a glass of orange juice. He is only a man eating a piece of bread and drinking a glass of juice. That's all he is. He's shorter than I remember him, but he still has beautiful teeth and he's wearing a polo shirt. He is a man in a polo shirt sitting in the shadows of her filthy kitchen eating a slice of bread and drinking a glass of juice in the fetid air.

Have you ever smelled a corpse?

So this is the one who, finding me alone in bed with Lucy—this simple eater of bread and drinker of juice—this is the one who will shoot me with a Glock 10mm or vice versa, I think to myself when he sees me in this apartment alone with her. I think incredulously to myself, for it doesn't seem at all possible that something so simple as a man drinking juice and eating bread could possibly be so fearsome as Lucy claims him to be. He is only a simple man, I say to myself, with a beautiful smile and a polo shirt eating a piece of bread and drinking a glass of orange juice, is all, I tell myself. So this is the one, I say to myself, looking at him as if he is suddenly inextricably woven into my own destiny, who is suddenly inextricably woven into my own destiny. It doesn't seem possible, I say to myself. It doesn't seem possible that this stranger whom I only vaguely know, shorter than I remember him, with a life trajectory completely different from mine, shall have his life trajectory intersect with mine, and thereby, at the moment of intersection, change everything. It's not possible, I say to myself. This man is way too innocent.

If you only knew him the way I know him, she says, looking at me incredulously.

What do you want out of life? I ask myself, watching him eat his bread so absentmindedly. Too hard to say, I say to myself, watching Matthew Gliss sit in the shadows amid the wreckage and debris of her messy kitchen, which like the Vet's and my own, for that matter, is absurdly messy. It's impossible to put into words just exactly what I want, I say to myself, watching Matthew Gliss in the shadows of her kitchen, but all of a sudden I desire a juice and a piece of bread. A glass of orange juice, I think to myself, and a piece of bread would be really quite lovely right now. Of all the things in the world I could possibly desire at this very minute, I tell myself, I desire nothing more than to be perfectly peaceful eating a slice of bread and drinking a glass of orange juice as calmly and absentmindedly as Matthew Gliss sits there now eating his bread, drinking his juice in the fetid air of her apartment. Have you ever smelled a corpse? That is the only thing, really, in all the world that I actually want, I tell myself, watching Matthew Gliss in the shadows of her kitchen.

My Lotus Flowers. They were my saviors. They lived in a lean-to hut along the river. They taught me about the pleasures of living flesh—the pleasures of my flesh. After being so long with the corpses in the field I wanted to become a corpse myself. I didn't want to go on with life. But my Lotus Flowers taught me to want life. I was grateful they could teach me about the pleasures of the living flesh. I loved my

Lotus Flowers. They loved me. There was no fooling in our relationship. It was very pure and honest. You could not fool what we had—me and my Lotus Flowers.

I look in the window at him sitting in shadows and laugh to myself at what she tells me. He can't be held responsible, she tells me in all seriousness. He has told me, she says to me in the heat of her bedroom, that he can't be held responsible for what may obtain if he catches you here in this bed with me. And she used that expression: for what may obtain.

He can't be held responsible for what may obtain so if you don't like a little risk feel free to leave. But if you can handle a little risk then I recommend you take a good look at his picture there behind the glass cabinet because if you ever see him in my apartment while we're in bed making love: Run, don't walk, or try to talk your way out of it but run like fucking hell. Those are her words exactly: run like fucking hell.

Where the hell, I say to her in all honesty just after we finished making love, am I supposed to run? This is such a small cramped place you have here.

It may be small but there's an exit right over there, she says, pointing her finger at the door in her kitchen. Run straight through that door and if he's blocking the door run straight through him, down the steps the way you came, get into your car, and take off as fast as humanly possible. Because, and trust me on this, he cannot be held responsible for what obtains here.

But I've only an AMC Hornet. By the way, I tell her, it's an old car and it only goes so fast.

Well, make it go as fast as it can go is what I advise, she says to me lying naked in bed just after I grin and bear it. Then there is that mysterious smile of hers that makes me so proud, that mysterious smile, and when he steps in on us I do what she advised: I run like hell all the way down the steps to my car. Run as fast as my legs will carry me. Run as fast as my legs move, him yelling: You think you can get away with this? You think you can keep going on like this behind my back and get away with this?

What might the neighbors think, yelling 'bullshit' at the top of his lungs.

No way you're getting away with this. Bullshit. Screaming, dragging me by my hair. Screaming, dragging, and then pulling that thing out—the damage it can do is incredible—yelling 'bullshit,' and there I am, running for my life running running.

AND WHEN I RETURN. he says: Thanks for this. Raising his juice glass, he smiles his beautiful smile at me. Plink. So I got him.

Thanks for this, I say. And then quietly, ever so quietly out his door.

I never intended for it to go this far. Never intended. My blood ax sitting so long in my apartment, so long collecting dust and rust, never intended. Not this. Never this. Never. Not ever.

DO YOU KNOW what the difference between you and me is? the Vet asks, switching his tape from *Die Meistersinger* to *Madama Butterfly* or the other way around.

Do you know, I tell him, you're wrong there. Believe it or not, you're wrong there. There is no difference.

Listening to his music, he switches from *Die Meistersinger* to *Madama Butterfly* and he asks: Do you know what the difference between you and me is?

The difference is only twenty-five years, I tell him.

The difference, he says, is corpses. He lights one cigarette off the other. Until you smell a corpse, he says, you'll never know what I live with.

When he mentions the word 'corpse' I politely excuse myself.

Lightning Source UK Ltd.
Milton Keynes UK
UKHW010040050719
345621UK00001B/178/P

9 780875 806297